a sweet celebrity romance

Dumbstruck

DANA LECHEMINANT

ISBN: 978-1-965106-02-0

First Print Edition: January 2025

Bow and Arrow Press

Dumbstruck:
left unable to speak due to shock or surprise

Hollywood Hot Scoop

Jonah James - Rising Star Falls Hard in Vegas

RIGHT BEFORE FILMING BEGAN for the highly anticipated big screen adaptation of the popular mystery novel, *Frosted Peaks*, male lead Jonah James was seen hitting the slots at the Bellagio in Las Vegas. Rumor has it James lost over a quarter million, which is sure to be a blow for the fan favorite. While not at A-list level yet, I have a feeling he'll keep rising higher until he's nearly at the same level of fame as the likes of Derek Riley. (But we all know no one will ever match Derek, who has yet to be seen since his recent breakup with Bonnie.)

With his role as the charismatic Logan Banks sure to boost his career, James will soon be back to the betting tables and living his best life in between his many projects. I don't know about you, but the chances of seeing Jonah James in person make me want to hang out in Vegas for a bit once filming wraps up! I wouldn't mind being his good luck charm. ;)

With filming well underway, we're doing our best to get our hands on some behind-the-scenes footage while we wait for *Frosted Peaks* to hit the screens! Or maybe just some footage of Jonah James looking scrumptious on set, am I right?

If you haven't taken our quiz yet, be sure to find out which Gabrielle Frost Mysteries character you are, and subscribe to ensure you don't miss any juicy Hollywood news! XO

chapter one

June

It is a perfectly normal reaction to hide from an attractive man when he walks into your store and not at all pathetic.

Okay, so I don't actually *know* if he's attractive because I only saw half his features before I hid behind the front counter. He's wearing a baseball hat and sunglasses, which immediately made me think of all those superhero movies where that is the go-to disguise for the insanely attractive heroes when they're trying to lie low. Maybe that's the reason I got so spooked—I don't like people who think they have to hide.

The irony of that...

Moving slowly, I poke my head over the top of the counter where I've been hiding ever since the guy walked into my hardware store. He's at the back with another guy, the pair of them perusing the power tools. Still wearing the sunglasses despite being indoors. Yeah, he's definitely hiding, and a niggling feeling in my belly tells me I know why.

Laketown, a place too small and sleepy for visitors except when we host the county's summer carnival (which won't happen for a few more months), has been plagued the last week by a film crew. You might think it would be exciting to have them here, a way to put our little town on the map, but most people—me included—would rather be left alone. The movie will bring nothing but trouble when it puts Laketown on the metaphorical map.

Exhibit A is at the back of my store. Based on this guy's jawline and fit physique, he's most likely Jonah James, the movie's male lead.

I don't generally pay attention to movies, and I wouldn't have cared who was in this one if it wasn't an adaptation of my friend Hank's book. I happen to be a major fan of his books, so when they announced the cast for the adaptation, I had to be sure Jonah was a good fit for the character, Logan. He's got the right look, but I have yet to pass judgment on his acting skills. I've been meaning to wander over to watch when they film in town, but I haven't had the chance yet.

The guy in the hat looks over in my direction, and I duck back down, hoping he didn't see me. He might be a regular customer, but if that's Jonah James standing in my aisle, this could turn ugly. From the little I read about him on the internet, he's not the kind of guy we want wandering around town. He's the lose-thousands-while-gambling type who probably thinks his money and fame mean he can do no wrong.

"Hello?" Whether it's the hat guy or his friend, the man who speaks has a smooth and clear voice, which annoyingly sparks a thread of attraction through my chest. *Please let it be the other guy*. I don't need to be attracted to a celebrity. Or anyone. "Is anyone here?"

If I stay silent, maybe they'll leave? I can't imagine what an actor would need from a hardware store anyway.

"Maybe they're in the back?" a different voice says, this one gruff and broad. It seems to better fit the other guy, who has tree trunks for limbs. The handsome one is also nice and muscular, but not to the extent of his buddy.

Personally, I prefer the more toned look over bulging muscles. My ex was a gym rat with two goals in life: to get as big as he possibly could and to keep me controlled with the threat of overpowering me. He was a winner for sure. I'm smart enough to know not every strong guy is going to be like him—I appreciate a good set of muscles as much as the next gal—but there's a limit to what I find appealing, thanks to the jerk I left long after I should have.

"Hello?" the smooth voice says again, suddenly much closer.

I tense, holding my breath. I'm a big girl, and I should help these guys with whatever they need and send them on their way, but at this point I'll look like I'm not fully right in my mind if I pop up and act like I wasn't hiding. *Great business practice, June.*

"Ahem."

My head shoots up, and I stare at the sunglasses that reflect my terrified expression. The guy is leaning over the counter and looking down at me with his lips twisted up in an amused smile. "Uh." I have nothing I can say that will explain why I'm sitting on the floor.

His smile grows. "You okay down there?"

Just act normal, June. "I, uh, it's my lunch break." Well that was a stupid response. No one eats lunch on the floor.

As if reading my thoughts, the guy turns his head to look at his big friend, who has joined him, then says, "Do you always spend your lunch break on the floor?"

I scramble to my feet and straighten the apron I'm wearing. "Maybe. What can I help you with?"

He purses his lips, a dimple forming on one cheek as he fights his growing smile. I still can't see his eyes, but I'm certain he's Jonah James. And he is *stupidly* attractive. It's almost criminal. "Is your lunch break over? I don't want to interrupt."

My stomach gurgles, loudly enough that the bigger guy furrows his brow, and I sigh. My already flimsy excuse is dead now. "I'm happy to help. What are you looking for today?"

"A set of Allen wrenches," the guy with trunks for arms says, leaning one of those massive arms on the counter and making me take a half step back. I don't mean to, but his build reminds me of my ex, and instinct can be hard to suppress.

My ex only hit me once, but it was enough to make me wary.

"You have metric," he continues, "but I need an imperial set if you have them."

The other guy—the pretty one in the hat—seems to be staring at me, making it difficult to think straight as I process what I'm being told. "Imperial? Oh, um, unfortunately I'm out. They've been on backorder for a couple of months, and no one usually..." I shouldn't finish that sentence. *No one usually buys things like that from me.* People in Laketown already have most of the tools they need, so they only come to me for things like nails and replacement bits for their drills. When I bought this place a couple of years ago, when I moved to town, I thought maybe it was rundown because the previous owner was too old for upkeep. It turns out he just didn't have much business.

The only reason I'll be in the black this month is because the film crew blew through here when they arrived and purchased a bunch of stuff to build their sets. It might be annoying to have them clogging up Main Street to film, but at least they added to my bank account.

"I said the same thing to that film crew," I add, shifting my gaze to the pretty boy and trying to judge his reaction.

He smiles broadly; it's practically blinding. "Film crew? That sounds fun."

He *has* to be Jonah. Guys as pretty as him don't come to places like Laketown for fun. And if he's Jonah James, that means he's an overpaid celebrity with a sense of entitlement that will render him completely obnoxious if I have to talk to him much longer. Fine, I don't know if he'll be obnoxious, but I can't imagine anyone with his level of fame will be anything but cocky and self-absorbed.

Putting my hands into my apron pockets so I can clench them into fists without the men seeing, I try to offer a neutral smile. "Yeah, they're filming some sort of mystery, but most of us can't wait for them to leave." I wait for any sign of offense—he gives me nothing—then turn back to the big one. "What are you working on? There might be a close enough metric wrench to get the job done, though you'll want to make sure you don't strip the bolt."

His smile is far less dazzling than his friend's, but it's kind. "Trailer door," he says with a shrug. "But yeah, I'm sure there will be one close enough. The door keeps sticking, so I'm trying to figure out where the problem is."

"Ah, I don't know enough about trailers to help you, but if the metric set doesn't work, you can return it." I gesture to the wrenches hanging near the back, glad that I've managed to sound civil despite my growing irritation.

The only trailers in town belong to the production crew. There's a slight chance these guys are passing through and have a camping trailer or something similar, but I doubt it. Why else would Pretty Boy still be wearing his sunglasses? I assume he doesn't want to be recognized in a place so far beneath him.

As the tree-limbed one heads back to the shelf to grab a set of wrenches, I study the other and ask, "Is it too bright in here?"

That gets a chuckle out of him, and he leans on the counter, putting himself obnoxiously close to me. He smells as good as he looks, and I hate that a part of me wants to close the gap between us even more. I've spent the last couple of years burying the part of me that takes an interest in anyone, but somehow this actor is digging it right back up with that charming smile. "I take it you're not a fan of the movie crew?" he asks in that smooth voice of his. It's such a clear, deep voice that it makes me shiver. "Have they been a problem?"

Even though people in town like to complain, the film crew haven't been problematic as far as I'm aware, other than disrupting the quiet status quo. But I roll my eyes anyway as I take the wrench set from the big guy and ring him up, glad for an excuse to put some distance between me and Pretty Boy even though we're still talking. "We like things to stay quiet here. If the movie does well, people will start flocking to Laketown."

"You think one movie could have that much influence?"

"I think there are enough fans of the book that they'll be coming in droves if the movie is good."

He rubs his jaw thoughtfully. "And what if the movie is bad?"

"Then I pity the actors who ruined a well-loved story."

Laughing, he stands up straight and claps a hand on his friend's shoulder. "Then we'd better hope the movie is good. Thanks for your help. Maybe I'll see you around...June."

As they head out, I glance down at the nametag pinned to my apron, wishing I had forgotten it this once. The last thing I need is a stuck-up movie star with a beautiful face taking notice of me. "Not likely," I say with a shrug and make a mental note to avoid the set whenever possible. "Good luck with your, uh, trailer."

Pretty Boy pauses at the door and looks back, using a finger to pull his sunglasses down and give me a good view of his golden-brown eyes. "Thanks," he says brightly and offers a smile so beautiful that I get weak in the knees.

Definitely Jonah James, and with the way my heart starts pounding in my chest after he leaves, I might have a problem on my hands. It's one thing to be attracted to a handsome guy; it's another thing entirely to be drawn to a movie star who will only be in town for a few weeks.

I turned off my heart when I left my ex two years ago, and somehow—seriously, how?—Jonah's smile just sparked it back to life.

CHAPTER TWO

JONAH

"Logan is the bad guy."

You know that feeling when someone says something that rocks your whole world view, and for a second you can't hear anything but a rushing in your ears as you process? I *hate* that feeling, which means I hate this moment as I stare at McAllister, the author of the book we're adapting into a movie. Logan, the character I've been playing as the charming hero and love interest, *is the bad guy*? McAllister had better be joking. I *need* him to be joking.

"Wait," I say, still in processing mode. "What? I am? Since when?" And *why* didn't someone tell me? My agent, the director, the casting director, *anyone*! Hurrying to the edge of set, where my assistant, Dexter, is waiting with the script, I snatch the pages out of his hands and flip through them, desperately searching for some sort of proof that the author is lying. If I've been acting this character wrong, I'm going to have fans of the books calling for my head, and there is nothing that terrifies me more than the threat of angry fans.

That's not true. I'm deathly afraid of sharks and small spaces, but disappointed fans are a close third.

My eyes land on a scene where my character reveals his true—clearly insidious—intentions, and I swear under my breath. The author is right. Of course he's right! He wrote the dang thing. And now my mind is running through all the scenes we've filmed so far and how badly I've portrayed my character.

This is bad. This is so bad.

"Jonah?" Dexter asks, sensing my rising panic.

This job was supposed to be my big break, to push me into the next level of acting and get me the kind of recognition that would solidify me as a solid hire. Now? Now it might be the thing that completely obliterates my career. "I need you to buy me that book," I mutter, still staring at the lines in the script that would have tipped me off if I'd had a chance to read the whole thing. As it was, I'm lucky I made it here on time to start filming.

"Which book?" Dexter asks.

I scowl at him. "Which one do you think?" Then I wince, hating how angry I sound. This isn't his fault. "Sorry. *Frosted Peaks*. Maybe buy the rest of the series too, while you're at it." I send him off with a clap on his back and return my focus to the script, skimming the last few scenes so I at least know how it ends.

I'd like to say I'm more professional than this—more prepared—but I rarely have time in between projects to read entire scripts. It hasn't been a problem before now because there's always someone to give me a good overview of my character. I glance at Beckett, a director I've worked with before, and narrow my eyes. He has given me nothing but praise for my work so far, even though my costar Bonnie usually has something to say about the scenes we're doing. Beckett always writes her suggestions off as inexperience, but I'm starting to think maybe she's the only one who has a grasp on the story we're telling.

My eyes jump to Bonnie. She's over by the author, a man she is supposedly dating according to a popular tabloid site, though both their body language looks anything but comfortable despite their inability to look away from each other. Not that it's any of my business. What *is* my business is the fact that I should have been listening to her from the beginning, and guilt winds its way through my body, leaving me tense.

I'm trying to be better at my job, but clearly I'm not doing well at that goal. I'm going to be stuck as a B-list actor forever, assuming I somehow manage to salvage the part I'm playing now. "Hooray for me," I mutter.

Boom!

A deafening noise reverberates through the street, and I duck as people scream. *What in the—*

"Jonah!" Richie comes barreling at me a second later, ready to tackle me to the ground and shield me with his giant body.

I hold up my hands, my eyes locking on the now-mangled front tire of the SUV we're using in the scene. "Hey, whoa, everything's—"

My bodyguard smashes into me, taking us both to the ground and knocking the wind out of me. "Stay down," he hisses, lifting his head to assess the damage. It's not normal for tires to explode out of nowhere like that, but...

"Richie," I choke out. He weighs a million pounds, and I can barely breathe. "I'm fine."

"I'll tell you if you're fine."

I'm not fine, but it has nothing to do with the tire and everything to do with the likelihood of me tanking this movie, just like that hardware employee the other day said it would. She didn't actually say I would be the reason it fails, but she clearly isn't rooting for this movie. Or me. And after McAllister watched the last scene we filmed, he seems to agree about my performance being wrong, which isn't exactly a glowing review.

I take a breath—not easy. "Rich?"

He looks down, his face only inches from mine. He must not have seen any threats, or he would have kept surveying the area. "What?"

If I'm going to be stuck here for a minute, I might as well make conversation. "Did you know Logan is the bad guy in this movie?"

His eyes go wide. "What? Since when?"

At least it's not just me. "Apparently since always."

"But you haven't—"

"I know." I grimace. "How likely would Beckett be willing to refilm everything we've done so far?"

Chuckling, he gets to his feet and grasps my hand, pulling me up with him. "The director who is notorious for wanting things his way? Good luck with that."

"Yeah, that's what I was afraid of." As Richie tries to brush dirt from my back—wardrobe won't be happy—I glance around the set to make sure no one got hurt. Everyone seems fine, if spooked, though Bonnie is suddenly looking cozy in McAllister's arms. Interesting...

"Could I get props over here?" Beckett, director extraordinaire, says into his megaphone. He seems thoroughly annoyed by the delay, though he should be more concerned about the fact that Bonnie and I were only moments ago standing right next to the now-deflated tire. "Everyone take a break. Bonnie, Jonah, let's run through the blocking again."

I frown at Beckett, who is already back to talking with another member of the crew. "We don't need blocking," I mutter, ducking under Richie's arm in search of some water and a moment to relax. "We need a new scene because I've been playing Logan all wrong." I find an unbusy crew member who stands at attention when I approach, her wide eyes making her appear mildly terrified.

"Do you need something, Mr. James?"

I'm regretting sending Dexter off to find me a book because he always anticipates my needs. I hate asking for things. "Some water, please?" I ask with a smile. She scurries off like I just threatened her job if she didn't find me water in the next thirty seconds, and I sigh. I'm no more important than she is, but I get this royalty treatment all the time, even at the level I'm at now. The more famous I become, the less human I feel.

It's the one part of my job I hate.

"Jonah James," a sharp voice says behind me.

I may have only talked to her once, but I still recognize June's voice. Grinning, I turn to face her and can't help but laugh when I catch sight of her scowl. "That's quite a greeting, June." And for some reason, seeing her has made me instantly relax. I have no idea why, with the way she's glaring at me. But after all that nonsense I just went through, I'm desperate for a change of pace, and June has given me the perfect avenue. She was barely civil to me at the hardware store, and it was hilarious. "And here I thought we might become friends."

"Ha!" She folds her arms. She's wearing the same apron she was the other day when I went into her store, and I have to wonder if she ever works or if she spends all her time hiding from customers and wandering Main Street. "You're part of the movie."

I fold my arms to match her. "Yes, I am."

"You could have said."

"Would it have made a difference?" I knew she recognized me, but I enjoyed her disdain more than I should have. My only regret is that I didn't flirt with her to see if it would make her mad, but she just gave me another opportunity.

Her scowl shifts to a glare, but though she opens her mouth, no words come out.

"Lunch break?" I ask, nodding in the direction of the hardware store.

She huffs. "Actually, yes."

"And you decided to spend it with us instead of on the floor? I'm touched." I'm not winning myself any favors by teasing her, but will that stop me? No. Her apparent dislike of me is a nice change from everyone catering to my every need.

As if on cue, the crew member from before stuffs an ice cold bottle of water into my hand right as I lift my hand to run it through my hair. It looks like I was anticipating the water, and I wince.

June scoffs as she eyes the bottle. "No, I'm here to support my friend." She nods toward Bonnie. Toward the *author*.

I take a drink of water, trying to judge from her scowly expression if this really is a friendship or if she doesn't like the way Bonnie is gazing at McAllister like he holds all the answers to the universe. "Friend, huh?"

Is this my pathetic way of ascertaining if June is single? Sure. But it's too dangerous to ask a woman outright. I've had way too many people latch themselves on to me in the hopes of capitalizing on my fame, so I never let anyone know if I'm available. Even if I am. *So* available.

I don't even remember the last time I had a good date.

To my delight, June scoffs again and shakes her head. "Hank is a friend, yes. Besides, the internet is pretty convinced he and Bonnie are already a thing."

I never believe a word websites like *Hollywood Hot Scoop* say. According to the tabloid, Bonnie and the author are the next big thing, but they also ran a story about me being in Vegas recently, and I wasn't even in Nevada. They don't always get things right. "Do you read a lot of tabloids?" I ask, folding my arms again to match her guarded stance.

"Of course not."

"So you haven't read about me?"

"Why would I want to do that?"

I laugh. Her contempt is weirdly refreshing, though I shouldn't be even more interested knowing she doesn't like me. That's a recipe for disaster right there. But something about her intrigued me the other day and hasn't gone away. "You tell me," I say. "You're the one who came to talk to me, remember?"

"Because I wanted you to know that I'm annoyed you didn't tell me who you are."

This woman is quickly becoming the most interesting person I've ever met, and I shake my head at her with a grin. "June," I say, leaning close once more, "I'm not the sort of guy who goes around introducing myself as a movie star."

"Sure you're not," she replies, rolling her eyes.

"Hi," I say, holding out my hand. "I'm Jonah James, popular actor and star of many a woman's fantasies. Nice to meet you." I snort out a laugh before I can get the last word out. "Is that how you think I should go about things?"

Though she grits her teeth and narrows her eyes, a smile plays at her mouth, and it's enough to give me a boost of confidence. "What kind of name is that, anyway?" she asks after a long moment of silence. "Jonah James. You sound like an outlaw."

I laugh. "You mean Jesse James?" Would it make her angrier if I told her that that's exactly where I got the idea for my stage name? Probably. "If I tell you my real name, will you like me better?"

"I don't care about your name." But the curiosity in her eyes says otherwise.

I could play with that. Though I shouldn't—it's not like we would ever become something more than casual acquaintances before I'm off to my next project—I smirk at her and head toward where we're filming. "If you're extra nice to me," I call back to her, "I might actually tell you what it is."

"Don't bother!" she calls back. But that curious look is still there, and I get the feeling this isn't the last I've seen of June the hardware girl.

But first... I need to try to save this movie so I can save my career.

CHAPTER THREE

JUNE

WHEN YOU GROW UP in a city like Denver, it's hard to imagine living in a town as small as Laketown, where there's a single traffic light and the mayor knows everyone by name. And then there's the privacy. Or lack of. Keeping a secret from your neighbors in a place like this requires being closed off and guarded.

Most of the time, I don't mind being the town's enigmatic spinster. All people know about me is that I rolled into town on fumes more than two years ago, bought the hardware store within a week of my arrival, and am content to stay single and independent.

I mean, it's not like there are any people to date in Laketown anyway. Hank is the only single man under the age of sixty, and while I love the guy, he's too academic for my tastes. Plus, he never leaves his house. The fact that he came to town the other day to see Bonnie is still blowing my mind. Even more surprising is the fact that he agreed to be Bonnie's fake boyfriend for publicity's sake.

He came to Laketown to hide from the world, just like I did, which is a huge part of the reason we became friends. And now that he's changing his tune, I'm left feeling unsettled. Unmoored. Which is ridiculous, because I could not possibly be more settled. I own a business and a house and a cat who may or may not hate me.

"Here, kitty," I say as I crouch down low on my porch with a can of tuna. I caught sight of the beast when I went to close the blinds in the front room, and I'm not one to miss an opportunity. "Tonight's the night you're going to let me touch you, right?"

I don't know why I bother. It's been six months since Samson first showed up in my bushes, and he's never once let me close enough to pet him.

"Come on, you fuzzball. It's time."

I can see him staring unblinkingly at me through the leaves, his squashed face catching the porch light. I have no idea what kind of cat he is other than orange and furry, but he keeps coming around, so I keep trying to turn him into a house pet so I can have some company after a long, quiet day at the store.

"I know you like tuna, big man," I tell him. "And I will gladly give you this whole can if you ask me nicely."

"Could I *pretty please* have the tuna?"

I shriek and scramble backward, realizing far later than I'd like that it wasn't the cat who spoke to me but the shirtless man standing on the sidewalk.

Jonah.

"What are you doing here?" I gasp, pressing a hand to my heart as if that might calm it down.

Smirking in his annoyingly handsome way, Jonah glances around my quiet street. "I'm on a run," he says, as if it should be obvious.

Maybe it would have been obvious if I'd gotten a chance to really study him. Tennis shoes, running shorts, and earbuds make up his entire ensemble, though I have no idea why he isn't wearing a shirt when it's maybe forty degrees out right now. I'm freezing just looking at him.

And look at him I do. I knew he was built, but Jonah James has some serious muscle definition. I shouldn't be surprised, given his resume, but he has managed to find that perfect in-between, plenty strong but not burly like his friend. He could keep a girl safe if she needed him to.

A shiver runs through me. Because of the cold. Not because I'm imagining a guy like Jonah stepping between me and a ready fist.

Samson rustles in the bushes and pokes his head out, curious about the half-naked man standing on my sidewalk.

"Oh hello," Jonah says, dropping into a low crouch. "I take it you're the tuna lover." To my surprise—and burning jealousy—Samson walks right up to Jonah and head butts his hand, leaning into his touch as Jonah scratches his back. "You're an ugly thing, aren't you?"

"How did you do that?" I gasp.

Jonah looks up. "Do what?"

"Samson has never once let me touch him."

"Huh. Can't imagine why not, with your friendly personality."

Scoffing, I stand and take a single step toward the two of them. Samson immediately darts back into the bushes, and my eyes inexplicably sting with tears. It's a *cat*. I don't even like cats! It shouldn't matter that this one likes the smug, pretty-boy actor but not me.

To my relief—disappointment?—Jonah grabs his shirt, which he'd tucked into the back of his shorts, and pulls it over his head. *Oh*. Not a shirt. A tank top that still shows off his well-defined arms. "In my defense," he says, "I'm a farm boy. The animals always tended to like me."

Shoot. That shouldn't make me like him more—I'm a city girl through and through—but it does. "Farm boy?" I ask, unable to keep the surprise out of my voice.

He laughs, and the sound seems to warm the air around us. "Why the tone of surprise? Is it because you can't read that on the internet?"

Oof, it's like he has access to my search history. Yeah, I may have looked him up a little bit after talking to him on the set the other day, but he doesn't have to be so cocky about being famous enough to have a Wikipedia page. Hank has one too, so it's not like it makes Jonah special.

"As if I would bother looking you up," I say.

Samson yowls in the bush like he's calling out my lie.

Jonah's smile shifts into a smirk again as his eyes flick to something behind me for half a second. He takes in the street once more and raises an eyebrow. "Quiet place."

I fold my arms, suddenly defensive of my tiny neighborhood. "I happen to like it."

"I never said I didn't."

Does he ever stop smiling? I can't decide if he's perpetually happy or if something about me amuses him, but either option unnerves me. I've gotten used to seeing the same people day in and day out, so I don't know how to act around this guy. He, on the other hand, gets paid millions of dollars to play pretend. I can't trust that any of his charm is real.

The last time I trusted a charming guy, he turned out to be narcissistic and manipulative. Besides, even if Jonah is genuine, he's only here until they're done filming, so I shouldn't drink in the way his muscles shift and stretch with each movement. I shouldn't wish he'd keep talking so we can spar like we did on the set the other day.

I shouldn't be itching to invite him inside before he freezes.

Something down the street catches Jonah's eye, and a wider grin stretches across his face. "Looks like my bodyguard has caught up to me, so I'll be on my way. I'll see you around, June."

"Don't count on it."

He chuckles and takes off running. A few seconds later, the trunk-limbed guy from the store huffs and puffs past, a look of desperation in his eyes as he gasps out Jonah's name and lumbers onward.

Samson yowls again.

"Oh, shut up," I tell him and leave the can of tuna on the step, heading back inside with no plans to hit play on the Jonah James movie I pulled up earlier.

Definitely not going to watch it.

Chapter Four

JONAH

"I DON'T UNDERSTAND WHY this keeps happening." Beckett runs his hands through his hair as he paces in the small on-set trailer we have in town. I get that he's frustrated, but the more he paces, the tighter this space is going to feel and the more I'm going to want to escape for the wide open skies outside.

I clear my throat. "Things go wrong. It happens."

Laughing, he gives me a wild look and doesn't slow his steps for a second. "I understand that things go wrong. It's part of filming a movie. But this is getting ridiculous!"

I have to agree with him, as much as I don't want to. What started out as a couple of accidents and malfunctions is turning into a pattern of safety issues and set disasters. I've seen my share of mishaps on set, but something about this movie has drawn more than normal.

A few days ago, one of the crew members said something about this movie being cursed. Most people laughed him off. But as things keep happening—like light bulbs going missing and furniture randomly falling apart, more and more people are starting to think he was right.

I'm not one to believe in curses or ghosts, but enough disasters have hit us that my convictions are feeling slippery. It's like someone said "Macbeth" instead of calling it "The Scottish Play," and the theater geeks are spooked.

I can believe in ghosts for a few weeks without it turning into a whole thing. Right?

"Okay, you have to stop," I say, grabbing Beckett's arm as he passes me. "You're making *me* nervous."

"It's Bonnie's fault." Beckett drops onto the couch next to me and drops his face into his hands. "She convinced me to change the script, and now I'm being punished."

I've known this guy for a while now, but I wouldn't have expected him to buy into the curse nonsense. He's too pragmatic for that, and I thought his confidence had no bounds, which is one of the reasons I try to work with him as often as I can. But I guess when a caterer comes across an entire crate of empty but intact eggshells that were fine the day before, it's difficult to toss the curse idea aside.

I have to admit, empty eggs are creepy.

The trailer door opens, and Bonnie comes inside with a bright smile. "Good morning!" she says but pauses when she sees Beckett hunched over. "Everything okay?"

"Great," Beckett says in a groan.

Meeting Bonnie's gaze, I shrug. "You ready for your big stunt today?"

Though she nods, Bonnie's smile is nervous. "So ready! My stunt double said she's been perfecting the stunt all morning and will show me how it's done before I try it out."

Good for Bonnie. Growing up on a farm, I got used to doing hard things, but I've grown soft over the years and rarely do my own stunts. If anything were to go wrong, I could get injured and be out of a job, and it's not like I have many skills outside of acting. I guess I could do voice-over work, but that's way less fun than being on the set and in the moment.

Not that it matters. I'm not jumping across a building like Bonnie's planning to. Maybe she shouldn't do it, if the set is cursed...

Okay, wow, I need some air, and Bonnie is staring at Beckett like she's worried he might fall apart. Time to run some interference. "I want to see Anne in action," I tell Bonnie, gesturing for her to lead the way outside to where her stunt double has been for the last couple of hours. As soon as we're out of earshot, I add, "There was an incident in catering this morning, so he's on edge."

"What kind of incident?"

The kind where normal eggs emptied of their contents overnight. I'm surprised she hasn't heard about it, but I'm guessing her new relationship with the author is keeping her attention. "Nothing too crazy, but you know how people are talking. So this is the rig you'll be in?"

As Bonnie talks me through the jump she's going to be making, my thoughts stray down the street to the hardware store like they've been doing pretty much nonstop since last night. More specifically, I'm thinking about the woman behind the counter inside. Coming across June's house last night was purely accidental. Seeing her in pajama pants and a messy bun was a happy side effect of that accident. Even dressed down like she was, something about her scratched an itch I didn't notice I had until I kept running and instantly wanted to turn back for relief.

The freeze frame image of my face on the TV behind her—visible through one of the front windows—got me wondering if she's more interested in me than she's pretending to be. Whether or not the two of us have potential, I plan to show June how interested I am.

It won't go anywhere, but it would be nice to have a little fun while I'm here.

"It should be fine, right?" Bonnie asks breathlessly.

Ah man, I didn't hear a word she said before that. "I'm sure," I say, hoping that's the answer she's looking for.

Thankfully, Bonnie smiles and nods like my assurance was all she needed. "Wish me luck!"

"Good luck," I say and pray she doesn't need it.

Twenty minutes later, disaster strikes. Bonnie makes the jump, but the rigging catches halfway between the two buildings. She jerks upward, and everyone gasps as it drags her higher. Fear shoots through me as I helplessly watch her keep rising until she comes to a sudden halt at the top of the crane. Dangling high in the air.

"Get her down!" Beckett shouts through the megaphone at the same time one of the assistant directors calls the fire department.

People start shouting, scrambling to find a way to help Bonnie, who is pale as a ghost but unharmed. What if the rigging breaks? What if she falls? I force a breath before panic overwhelms me, but there's nothing I can do to help.

I swear under my breath, but Bonnie's bodyguard appears, shoving his way through the gathered crew until he's directly beneath Bonnie. He won't be able to do much but slow her fall, but at least he's there.

"It's the curse," someone whispers.

"There's no such thing as curses," I whisper in return, more to myself than anything. I rub my jaw and squint up at my costar, wishing I had a way to help her. I can't just stand here and wait...

In my search for a way to be helpful, I find Beckett under a canopy and breathing into a paper bag.

"Whoa," I say, patting him on the back. "You good?"

"I knew it!" he says. "I angered some long-dead spirit by letting Bonnie touch the script, and now it's attacking the movie and trying to get rid of her."

I can't decide if I prefer ghost over curse, but I'm pretty sure Beckett's losing it. "Dude, will you calm down? It's just a technical problem." I *hope* it's just a technical problem.

"What if she falls?" Beckett groans and returns to breathing into the bag. I didn't think people actually did that, but he is a pro at bag-breathing. "What if she falls from the rigging and dies? Or is disfigured? Have you seen how many people are talking about Bonnie Aiken right now? This film will be ruined, and we'll have to shut down, and I'll never make a movie again because I'll be the guy who got Bonnie Aiken killed by an angry ghost!"

His panicking is doing nothing to help the whispers circulating among the crew, but something in his spiral sparks a thought. What if someone—a real someone, not a ghost—is trying to shut down the movie? People in this town haven't been quiet about how much they hate us being here—even June said as much.

Leaving Beckett to his hyperventilating, I slip through the panicked staff and down the alley Bonnie's dangling over, making my way to the crane that lifted her up. The two operators who are running the thing look terrified as they whisper back and forth, and neither looks confident that they'll be able to fix the problem.

"Can you get her down?" I ask.

Both men jump and stare at me. "Oh! Mr. James. Um, we're working on it as fast as we can."

"Any idea what caused the malfunction?" I don't know why I'm asking. I'm far from a mechanical whiz, and I never even drove the tractor back at home because Dad knew I wouldn't be able to fix it if something went wrong in the middle of a field. I stuck to horses, though I can't claim to be a horse whiz either.

I'm not a whiz at anything. Jack of all trades, here. Some trades. A few trades. Blegh.

If it were me in that rigging and I fell, I have no idea what else I could do with my life. Assuming I survived. And that's a terrifying thought, one that makes me think I should get in touch with my agent and make sure my schedule is fully booked next year.

"Well…" One of the operators fiddles with a switch while the other shields his eyes to look up at Bonnie, who seems fairly calm given her situation. Her assistant is shouting something to her, and she waves back at him. "We think it might be a…"

I lift an eyebrow when he doesn't finish his sentence. "A what?"

"We have no idea what caused it," the other man says with a sigh. "But we're working on it."

"It must be something in the wiring," the first guy says. "But it was fine an hour ago."

"Get her down," I tell them and head back toward Beckett's canopy. I don't have any sort of power over the crew, but the two men renew their efforts with more vigor, so I'll call that a win.

When I get back to the main commotion, no fewer than four people—Richie included—shuffle me away from the crane and tell me to stay somewhere safe, like I might be the next victim. It's ridiculous, but a part of me shares their worry, so I move to the edge of the street to watch in concern.

I'm helpless, and I hate that feeling.

I need a distraction before I start coming up with questionable plans to rescue Bonnie. No one needs me climbing up the crane to try to help her out of the harness. Not that Richie would ever let me get that far.

Dexter finds me a moment later, thankfully providing me with the distraction I need. "I got that info you were wanting, Jonah!"

"Finally some good news!" I wrap an arm around his shoulders and walk us to an awning overhanging the sidewalk so we're relatively alone. "Tell me everything."

"Her name is June Harper," Dexter says proudly. Yeah, okay, I shouldn't have sent my assistant digging, but I couldn't help it. "Moved here a couple of years ago. She used to work for a district attorney in Denver before she bought the hardware store here in Laketown from the old guy who owned it before. She hasn't dated anyone since coming here, and the only person she talks to is the author, McAllister."

"June and the author aren't dating, are they?" What was the guy's first name? Henry, according to the tabloids, but Bonnie calls him Hank.

Dexter shakes his head. "Nope. McAllister never leaves his house."

"Except when he and Bonnie are out on a date." During my run last night, I ran past the ice cream shop here in town and saw the two of them sitting cozy in a corner booth. There might be more truth to the *Hot Scoop* articles about their relationship than I originally thought. "Okay, so she owns the hardware store?" That's impressive. "Any idea why she left Denver?"

"Because the city left a bad taste in my mouth," a feminine voice says behind me.

I whirl around, tongue sticking to the roof of my mouth as I realize I've been caught. I recover quickly, flashing her a smile even though she looks none too happy to see me. "June Harper."

"How did you find all that out?" she asks Dexter.

Dexter turns a deep shade of red, which is impressive. Not much can stun him, but it seems June has slipped under his skin with a single question. "Oh, um, well, I asked around."

Letting out a heavy sigh, June closes her eyes, like she's praying for patience. "This town..."

"I think this town is charming outside of its ghosts," I say.

She opens her eyes, brow furrowing. "Ghosts?"

I nod toward Bonnie. "Apparently we're being haunted."

"That's not a..." She trails off as she seems to realize what she's looking at. "Is that why everyone is freaking out? Is she stuck up there?"

"Something went wrong with the crane, and no one can get her down."

"Poor thing."

"Oh! That's not good," Dexter says. "Has anyone called 911?"

"Maybe go check on that." I give him a narrow-eyed look that he properly interprets, nodding once before scurrying away and leaving me alone with June. "I'm sorry I had him look into you," I tell her, though I'm not sure I mean it. "You can't fault a guy for being curious."

"Maybe not, but I can fault him for using small town gossip as a reliable source."

"Was any of the intel wrong?"

It seems to cause her a great deal of pain to admit, "No."

"I think it's sexy that you own the store," I tell her. "And now it makes sense how you can leave whenever you want." I tug at her apron.

Call me crazy, but her glare is magnetic. And it's so unlike the looks I usually get that I'm desperate for more of it, even if that means making her dislike me even more than she already seems to. Glutton for punishment over here.

"Do you ever actually do your job?" I ask her.

She rolls her eyes. "Not when you're around."

"Hate to break it to you, Harper, but this is twice now that you've approached *me*. I don't think I can carry the blame here." I'm not reading too much into things, am I? If she really hated me, she'd simply avoid me.

June huffs and folds her arms, shifting so she's standing shoulder to shoulder with me. She doesn't have to stand so close, but her arm is nearly touching mine. "I wanted to see what the commotion was all about."

"Well, now you've seen." And I wish I could do something about said commotion. Bonnie doesn't deserve to be stuck thirty feet in the air. Forty? It's high. But I'm stuck as a spectator, which means there's not much I can do but study the woman next to me who seems so determined to be cold and distant but is choosing to hang around.

Right as I'm about to open my mouth, someone calls out June's name.

She turns, eyebrows lifting in surprise, and takes a few steps forward. "Hank!"

The author. I'm not sure I like this guy.

"What's going on?" he asks. "Someone said Bonnie is stuck up there."

"It was a malfunction," I say, matching June's steps so we're standing next to each other again. "They're working on getting her down."

Hank narrows his eyes as he looks at me. We haven't officially met, though we talked the other day, and he seems as wary of me as I am of him. Granted, he's the one who told me I had my character all wrong, so I'm guessing he doesn't have a high opinion of me at the moment. In my defense, I read his entire book over the last few days—stayed up later than I should have to get to the end—and am halfway through the next book because his storytelling is compelling.

"Has anyone been able to talk to her?" Hank asks June.

Once more, I'm the one who answers because June just got here. "Her assistant has been shouting at her."

Hank frowns at me and once more talks to June. "That must be awful for her. June, do you still have those walkie talkies?"

"Oh! Good idea. Let me go grab them."

I don't want to stand here and be judged by the author, so I follow June, something she doesn't realize until I grab the open door of the hardware store as she's stepping inside.

"I don't need your help, Jonah James," she says as she rounds the front desk to the other side.

"Do you always call people by their full names?" I ask.

She rolls her eyes as she digs in a drawer. "When they are egotistical and self-important celebrities, yeah."

"Huh. Tell me if you meet one of those because they sound awful."

It's a small victory, but she smiles, shaking her head as if she can't believe I broke her hard shell with that one. She pulls out a couple of walkie talkies and fiddles with the knobs and buttons. "You are something else, James."

"That's what I hear. How can I help?"

Her eyes jump to me, and the surprise in her expression hits me square in the chest. Or maybe it's the way she is making eye contact for longer than half a second. Last night was our longest conversation so far, but most of the time she avoided looking at me. Still haven't decided if that was because she liked what she saw or didn't, but I'm hoping for interest rather than disgust.

I put in a lot of work to look this good, and it might wound the ego if she doesn't appreciate the effort.

"You...want to help?" she asks, as if nothing in the world could be more surprising to her.

Either I made a horrible first impression, or she's generally not fond of people she doesn't know. Choosing to ignore the hurt that comes from her unspoken judgment, I nod. "It may come as a shock, but I do want to make sure my costar is okay."

"Oh. Right. Well, there are some batteries on the wall in that back corner. Double A. We need four of them."

"On it." I remember seeing the array of batteries when I was here the first time, so it doesn't take long for me to grab a pack and bring it back to her. Though I offer the package, I pull it out of her reach when she tries to grab it. "For a price."

June sighs heavily. "You're going to make me pay for my own batteries?"

"Yep. With a date."

Her whole expression drops, like she's so surprised that I would suggest something like that that she has no idea how to react. "A date?"

"With me," I confirm. "Lunch, specifically, unless you've already taken your break today." This time, I set the batteries in her outstretched hand but hold on to them. It's not quite holding hands, but this is closer than I've gotten to her so far. There's some skin-to-skin contact going on.

Wrinkles form on her brow, and her confusion is cute. "You...want to take me to lunch? At ten in the morning?"

I shrug. "Of course I want to take you to lunch, June Harper. And I have no idea when you take your lunch break because it seems to happen at random times. I won't have a break until later anyway, but I'm willing to pivot if lunch is off the table today. Dinner, dessert, or even afternoon tea are acceptable alternatives."

She waits for so long that I'm convinced she's finding a way to turn me down, but when she finally speaks, it's not an answer to my request. "I should get these to Hank." Her hand slips free of mine, and she opens the batteries and stuffs them into the walkie talkies. She leads the way out of the store and back down the sidewalk.

Part of me wants to keep pushing, but I'm sensing a need to step back. Give her a little space to process. There are any number of reasons why she might say no, and though I'm determined to give her every reason to say yes, I have never been a typical aggressive male. I get the sense June wouldn't like that even if I was.

I can be patient.

"Here, Hank," June says, handing the walkie talkies to him.

Hank immediately waves Trevor, Bonnie's assistant, over and gives him the other radio. "Get this to Bonnie." Then he looks up at the building next to us, a determined glint in his eyes before he slips down a narrow alley and disappears.

"Where's he going?" I ask.

June smiles in a way that makes me wish she was smiling at me. It's a look of pride, something I don't get often now that I don't live on my parents' farm. Praise? Sure. All the time. But pride is a whole different beast. "I think he's going up to the roof," she says.

"Huh. Good idea." This building isn't quite as high up as Bonnie is across the street, but it'll give Hank a better view of her. "So are those two really dating?"

June's eyes go wide. "What? Of course they are. Why would you ask something like that?"

I shrug, noting the way she has gotten defensive. "They *say* they are, but I know a publicity stunt when I see one. Granted, they've had their moments over the last few days, but Bonnie didn't mention Hank once until after the first tabloid article dropped about the two of them. And Bonnie's chatty to the extreme, so I would have heard something about the guy if they were a thing, you know?"

I'm rambling. It's not a common thing for me, thank goodness, but that doesn't change the fact that I'm talking way too much if I want June to agree to go out with me. Tucking my hands into my pockets, I lift my shoulders in another shrug. "You don't have to tell me if you know something. I'm just throwing my opinion out there."

June raises an eyebrow as she studies me. "You're something else, Jonah James."

I chuckle. "So you've said."

"When...uh...when do you get a break?" She blushes and drops her eyes to the sidewalk. For all the snark she's given me, I wouldn't have expected shyness, and I take a small measure of hope from her timidity. If she wasn't interested, she would say so. "And why would you want to go to lunch with *me*?"

Oh, she might regret asking that second question, but I'm going for full honesty. "Depends on how quickly we can get Bonnie down, but we usually break for lunch around noon. And I want to go to lunch with you because I think you're beautiful and you're the first woman I've met in years who makes me feel normal."

"You think I'm…"

Okay, so I've literally left her speechless. That's fun. Grinning, I start walking backwards. "So, would you like to join me?"

"I…"

"Yes or no, Harper. Easy question to answer."

"Jonah…"

"Lunch?"

"Okay."

Resisting the urge to fist pump, I nod to acknowledge her response and then turn and walk away before I do or say something stupid to change her mind. People are still running around, trying to get Bonnie down, but she looks much happier now that she has a walkie talkie to talk to her maybe real boyfriend.

I locate Dexter among the crew and gesture him toward me. We've got a date to plan.

CHAPTER FIVE

JUNE

JONAH BOOKED OUT THE entire diner so we wouldn't have people whispering about us while we ate. It's weird to see this place empty—it's one of two restaurants in town and a popular spot at lunchtime, especially on a Friday like today—but it's even weirder to have the whole staff stare at me as I sit in a booth and wait for Jonah to show up. Dexter said the actor stopped by his trailer to change and will be here any minute, but I'm counting the seconds.

I'm starting to understand why Hank hates coming to town. These stares are getting ridiculous. Most people leave me alone, knowing better than to pry into my past after I spent a lot of energy shutting them down when I first moved here. But now that I'm here on my own, with no other townsfolk to distract them, I seem to be a point of interest once more.

Karina, one of the servers, wanders up to me after I've been sitting here for five minutes. "Well hello there, June," she says, her smile forced as she places a cup of water in front of me. "We wondered who got cornered by that actor, and I didn't expect to see someone like you walking through that door."

'Cornered' isn't necessarily the word I would use. Yeah, he surprised me when he asked me out, but I was too intrigued to say no. I'm woman enough to admit that much. "How much did he pay you to keep everyone else out?" I ask and take a drink of water to give myself something to do.

Karina snickers, glancing back at the others—two cooks who man the kitchen and another server. "Thousand dollars."

I choke on the water. "What?"

"Yep. For two hours."

Jonah James paid them a thousand dollars for a date with me? "Why would he do that?" I ask out loud.

It's a rhetorical question, but Karina still answers. "I'd expect because he likes you, June."

She'd better lose that bitter edge to her voice. If she's jealous, that's not my fault. It's not like I *wanted* Jonah to ask me out. "He doesn't even know me," I argue.

"Well, whose fault is that?"

I can't stop myself from glaring at her. "I'm good with water for now," I tell her. "Thanks."

Scoffing, Karina catches the hint and goes back behind the counter to whisper to Peg, the other server. I don't hear much of what they say, but I do catch enough to know they're talking about how they can't understand why Jonah would take an interest in *me* of all people.

Because I think you're beautiful and you're the first woman I've met in years who makes me feel normal. That's what he said. While I probably can't trust an actor, I do think he was being genuine. I watched a little bit of the scene they were filming after they got Bonnie down—I *really* hope Jonah has no idea I was there—and he's good at what he does. Now that he knows he's playing the villain, he has upped the subtle creepiness of his character. Fans are going to eat him up.

I shouldn't get a tingle of jealousy thinking about his fans, but I do. If he was telling the truth, he likes that I haven't treated him like a celebrity, which hopefully means he isn't as egotistical as I always imagine actors to be. Bonnie seems okay, especially because she's the only person who has ever gotten Hank to take a step toward healing after his traumatic past. Maybe Jonah is okay too.

It would be easier to get rid of that *maybe* if he would show up...

After fifteen minutes of sitting by myself, I ask Karina to bring me a soda. Half an hour after that, I order a plate of fries and wonder if I should leave. I get that filming a movie can be unpredictable, but it's not like the diner is far from the set. If he couldn't make it to lunch, he could have come and told me. Or even sent his assistant. A crew member. *Anyone.*

After sitting by myself for an hour, I ask Karina to bring me a BLT to go so I can head back to the store and berate myself for thinking the best of Jonah James. She and Peg both give me pitying looks that have a hint of 'I told you so' underneath, even though neither of them told me anything, but I can guess they're like the rest of the Laketownians who can't wait for Jonah and the others to pack up and head back to California.

I'm right there with them. What a waste of an hour.

When I get outside, sandwich in hand, I'm ready to wash my hands of the handsome and intriguing actor and stick to my solitary single life. But I only make it halfway down the block when I run into Dexter.

"Oh hey!" he says, then frowns when he looks behind me. "Is Jonah not with you?"

I scoff. "Jonah? You mean the guy who never showed up?"

To my surprise, Dexter turns pale. "He didn't show up?" Scrambling, he grabs a radio at his hip and says, "Does anyone have eyes on Mr. James?"

Nerves bubble up in my stomach, along with a healthy dose of guilt. "Is something wrong?"

Dexter purses his lips as he waits for a response on the radio, which never comes. "Something might be wrong," he says weakly and pulls his phone out of his pocket, dialing a number and lifting it to his ear. After a few tense seconds, he swears and dials a different number. That call seems just as fruitless. "Richie's went straight to voicemail," he says with a frown.

"Richie?"

"Jonah's bodyguard."

"What does that mean?" And is Laketown suddenly about to get a lot more attention because something bad has happened to one of Hollywood's hottest men? (That's an internet superlative, not mine. Even if it's true.) "Dexter, where is Jonah?"

Dexter moans and starts walking, and I stay hot on his heels, curiosity getting the better of me. "The last time I saw him, he was heading back to his trailer. Richie was supposed to bring him right back for his date with you. He never came?"

I roll my eyes despite the seriousness of the situation. "Does it look like he came?"

He climbs into a golf cart and gestures for me to join him. Though I hesitate, I want to know why I got stood up, so I decide to go along with him for now. As soon as I'm settled, he hits the accelerator and heads for the field where the film crew stays. "I guess we start at his trailer? It's the stupid curse..." He mutters that last part almost too quietly for me to hear.

I frown. "Curse?" Jonah mentioned something about the set being haunted earlier, but I thought he was joking. "What curse?"

Dexter shrugs as he drives. "There are always things that go wrong with a movie, but this one is way worse than any I've seen. People are starting to think we've upset some angry spirits."

"There's no such thing as ghosts." Unless you count the traces of trauma that never go away, of course, which is a different thing entirely. "What else has gone wrong?"

Dexter lists off more things than I expected him to, from missing props to spoiled food, and the more he talks, the more my gut tells me this is more than just accidents. It's not a ghost—that would be ridiculous—but someone is certainly angry.

In this town, it could be anyone. There are too many locals who think the movie is going to bring nothing but trouble when people realize Laketown exists.

Stopping outside a large trailer in the field the film crew has taken over next to the high school, Dexter hurries up to the door and knocks. "Jonah? Are you in here?" He stands tense as he waits for an answer.

Nothing.

"Jonah!" He tries the door, which opens with a little bit of sticking—I wonder if they ever found a wrench to fit—and pokes his head inside. "Jonah, you here?" He steps into the trailer, leaving me standing awkwardly in the dirt outside.

I was here not too long ago, helping Hank figure out a contract with Bonnie related to their staged relationship, and I feel even more out of place now than I did then. The few people who are walking around the tent- and trailer-filled space give me querying looks as they pass, with plenty of suspicion in their eyes.

Based on some of the things Dexter told me, I don't blame them for being wary of locals.

"His phone is here," Dexter says, coming back down the steps and making me feel less like a trespasser. "But he isn't."

I frown. "What does that mean?"

"I don't know." And he clearly doesn't like not knowing. His eyes dart around the field, full of worry, as he practically cradles Jonah's phone. "Jonah, where are you?"

After a moment of tense silence, we decide to try heading back into town to see if he somehow passed us without us noticing. But we only make it halfway across before Dexter slams on the brakes and points to an unattended golf cart parked near a small box trailer.

"That's the one Jonah uses," he says, scrambling out of his seat. "Jonah? Jonah!"

It's only when we approach the trailer that I hear a reply. "Dex?"

Dexter's eyes go wide, and he rushes to the trailer. "Jonah?"

Jonah's voice is muffled, but he's most definitely inside the enclosed trailer. "Dexter, you beautiful man. You found me!"

"Jonah, you were supposed to be back in town over an hour ago!"

Jonah barks out a laugh. "Trust me. I am well aware."

"What are you doing in the props trailer?"

"The door is stuck," Jonah says. "And Richie is freaking out. Ow!"

Dexter frowns. "Jonah?"

"That was uncalled for, Rich. But okay, I'm the one freaking out. Get us out of here, Dex. I'm begging you."

"He's claustrophobic," Dexter mutters to me as he reaches for the door and tugs to no avail. "He once got stuck in an airplane bathroom and hasn't been the same since."

That's...adorable. I shouldn't be thinking that—Jonah's allowed to feel fear without judgment—but I like knowing Jonah James isn't perfect. That there's something human about him.

"Who are you talking to?" Jonah asks. "And I'd better not have heard you talking about the airplane bathroom."

"He's talking to me," I say, putting my hand on Dexter's shoulder so I can take his place at the door. I doubt I'll do much better with getting the door open, but I figure I might as well try. I'm going to guess it's locked.

"June?" The tone of Jonah's voice shifts to something more desperate. "June, I swear I would have been on time if not for that door getting stuck."

"I'll believe it when I see it, Jonah James."

"If you get me out of here, I'll tell you my real name so you can stop calling me that."

The door is going nowhere, so I step back and turn to Dexter. "Who has a key for this thing?"

He shrugs. "Probably Myrna? She's in charge of the props. But she's in town with everyone else. I've never heard Jonah's real name..."

I snicker, even though I should focus on getting Jonah out of his predicament. If he really is claustrophobic, this is not the sort of place he should be for long, and he's probably been in there for at least an hour. "Sounds like it's prized information. Jonah, how did you get stuck in there in the first place?"

There's some sharp back-and-forth whispering inside, and then Richie—I think—says, "The ghost locked us in."

"No," Jonah says on a groan. "It wasn't a ghost."

"But it was!" Richie insists. "I heard her!"

That piques my interest. I'm not a believer in the supernatural, but whatever Richie heard could be helpful in figuring out what happened. "You heard the ghost?"

"We heard *something*," Jonah says. "Right before someone closed the door behind us. There's no evidence that points to a ghost. Any updates on getting me out of here, Harper? Dexter? *Anyone?*"

"What kind of something?" Dexter asks.

"She said we should leave," Richie says. "Sounded like a banshee."

"Banshees scream," Jonah says. "They don't give people orders."

"It was a ghost!"

Leaving them to their bickering, I search the vicinity as if I might find a way to get them out of the trailer. Most likely, Dexter will need to go back into town to find this props person and— "Oh!" I say, catching a glint of silver in the dirt. I pick up the key on its little ring and tilt my head, wondering if it was really that easy.

Sure enough, it fits the lock on the side door, unlocking it and letting me pull it open to reveal Jonah lying on his stomach on the floor, his head turned toward us and his eyes brimming with relief. Richie steps over him and makes his escape, but Jonah doesn't move.

He looks exhausted, and I wonder if Dexter wasn't kidding about Jonah having claustrophobia. Not that I thought it was a joke, but it looks like Jonah just had the worst hour of his life.

Maybe it's a bad idea, but I opt for a joke. "You stood me up, Jonah James."

He manages a weak smile. "Sorry. Can I make it up to you? Maybe not today. Monday?"

I pretend to think about it, but it's an easy answer. His vulnerability right now as he lies on the dirty trailer floor, sweaty and disheveled, is a good look for the Hollywood heartthrob. "I suppose I could give you one more chance," I say.

Jonah's smile is so genuine that I understand why he earned the title of heartthrob in the first place. He's giving me all sorts of feelings in my chest, feelings I haven't felt in a long time. He pushes himself up to his hands and knees and crawls over to sit in the doorway. Even in his post-panic state, he's impossibly handsome, and there's something new in his eyes that puts a crack in my shield that might be too big to ignore: remorse. Not only did he apologize for missing our date, but he genuinely feels bad about it and is taking responsibility when he doesn't need to.

My ex apologized all the time, but he never meant it.

Jonah means it.

"I owe you my name," he says.

"Do I get to hear it too?" Dexter asks.

Oh, I forgot he was standing right behind me.

Jonah chuckles and shakes his head. "Sorry, Dex. Gotta keep some secrets from you or you'll literally run my life."

"I already run your life," Dexter grumbles and heads over to the golf cart, flopping into the driver's seat.

"You should tell him your name," I say at the same time Jonah stands and comes to my side.

He chuckles. "Maybe. Eventually. But I like having one or two secrets that he doesn't know." Moving slowly, he reaches up and brushes some hair out of my face. I think the slow speed of his movement is as much from hesitation as it is from his exhaustion. He's being so careful, for which I am grateful.

My body is suddenly on high alert, and I can't tell if I'm excited or terrified. The feelings are eerily similar, and I hate this uncertainty.

"If I tell you my name," he says, "do you promise to keep it a secret?"

I tilt my head. "Is your name that bad?"

He chuckles and drops his hand, shaking his head. "You are determined to keep me humble, aren't you?"

"Someone should."

Grinning, he takes a step back, which is not what I expected. Then another. "You know what? I think I'll wait. Make you earn my name."

Disappointment floods through me. Wait, *disappointment*? I don't care what his name is. I don't even care about getting a rain check on today's lunch. So why does my heart ache a little bit more with each step he takes? "Didn't I just do that by rescuing you?"

He shakes his head. "Technically, yes. But something tells me I can leverage this information."

"What do you want?" And why am I even entertaining the idea of giving him whatever he asks for?

"Ice cream," Jonah says, still walking backward as he heads toward the other golf cart, where Richie is waiting for him. "An ice cream date Monday night after we're done shooting."

Does he plan on renting out the ice cream parlor as well? The Laketownians might riot; they love their ice cream. "What if I'm busy?" I ask.

"Your store closes at seven, so you have no excuses."

He knows my store hours? While that's adorable, I refuse to let him know he's getting past my defenses every time I see him. Narrowing my eyes, I pretend to consider his offer like I did before. "I don't know…"

Jonah grins and shakes his head. "Nah, that's not going to work, Harper. You agreed to give me a chance, so I know you're interested. Monday at eight. I'll be the one with a dozen roses and a charming smile."

"You think highly of yourself, don't you, Jonah James?"

He doesn't answer, instead hopping into the cart and letting Richie drive him away.

Dang, if he isn't as charming as he seems to think. What gets me is the fact that he doesn't come across as cocky in the slightest. It's just confidence. And there is nothing sexier than confidence.

But there's no way I can let him know that.

"I can take you back," Dexter says from the other golf cart.

I make my way to the cart but pause before sitting down, gazing at the key in my hand. It's extra shiny, like it was just made. Handing it to Dexter, I slide onto the seat and frown at the trailer. "Why would someone lock Jonah in a props trailer? Why was he in there in the first place?"

Shrugging, Dexter looks down at Jonah's phone, which he still has. "Looks like Myrna texted him and asked him to grab something for the next scene because she forgot it."

"Would Myrna have set him up?" And what purpose would that serve outside of being a mean prank?

"Nah, she *loves* Jonah. Everyone does."

I scoff. "There's no way *everyone* loves Jonah."

But Dexter shrugs again, a smile lighting up his face as he turns on the golf cart. "If there's anyone who doesn't like him, I haven't met them. I've worked for a few different celebs, and none of them come close to Jonah. He's good about making everyone around him feel valued and important. And if it makes a difference, I've never seen him act the way he acts around you. I think he really likes you."

"He doesn't know me," I mutter as we head back to town. But maybe it wouldn't be such a bad thing if I changed that fact.

CHAPTER SIX

JONAH

On Dexter's recommendation, I did not pay the ice cream parlor to have the place to myself, and I am regretting that with every passing second. Richie is just as bothered by the many stares I'm getting, and when Richie is nervous, I get nervous. And when I get nervous, I get sweaty. A first date is not a time to be sweaty.

"Maybe she's not coming," I mutter, tapping my fingers on the table in front of me. Honestly, I'm surprised June agreed in the first place after I missed our first date attempt. Okay, technically she didn't agree. But she also didn't say no. Because I didn't give her the chance. I doubt I made a great impression when she got the trailer door open and found me lying face down on the floor.

I'd stupidly forgotten my phone in my personal trailer in my haste to get back to town, and Richie is notoriously bad at letting his battery die. Which, honestly, is something we should fix. But as soon as I realized we were stuck inside the props trailer, panic set in, and I thought for sure I would be trapped there for hours.

Someone from set would have heard us eventually, and Dexter is good at keeping tabs on me, even when I don't want him to. But it's hard to think logically when you're trapped in a few square feet of space.

I was a mess, but June still didn't say no.

Groaning, I drop my head onto the table and do my best not to relive every interaction I've had with June. Honestly, it's been impossible to do my job the last few days because I keep thinking about her. That, and things are still going wrong on set. With all the disasters threatening the stability of my career, I hoped I could at least count on June. "I think I messed this up, Rich."

"Already?" a female voice says. "I just got here."

My head snaps up, adrenaline surging through me at the sight of June in a sweater and jeans standing next to the booth I picked. She's *beautiful*. As always. That's not going to help the sweating situation. "You came," I practically whisper. Talk about pathetic, but I am both relieved and terrified, which is a lethal combination.

June's lips twitch as her eyes shift to the bouquet of red roses sitting on the table. "I seem to recall you promising a charming smile to go with those."

My grin is fully natural as I stand and present the flowers to her. "You're going to have to decide if I live up to the charming part, but these are for you."

Someone loudly clears their throat in the next booth over, which a moment ago had been empty but now is occupied by three middle-aged women who are all giving me judgy stares, as if flirting with the resident hardware expert is an egregious error on my part.

I clench my jaw and try to keep smiling as June accepts the flowers. If I'm lucky, she's not set on this ice cream thing. "Maybe," I say, keeping my voice low, "we could go on a walk instead?" I subtly nod toward our irritated audience.

Richie clears his throat. After the trailer-trapping on top of everything else happening on set, he has been convinced someone is out to get me, and he's not thrilled about the idea of me wandering around town.

I ignore him and offer my hand to June. "What do you say?"

She looks at the women behind me, then nods and reaches for my hand. "Sounds great. I'm not big on ice cream anyway."

I hiss dramatically and pull my hand back. "That might be a deal breaker, Harper. Where am I supposed to take you out next time if you don't like ice cream?"

Rolling her eyes, she grabs my hand and pulls me out the door. "You are ridiculous, Jonah James."

I wait until we've walked most of the block and turn onto a quiet side street before I shift our hands, lacing our fingers together. "I hope I'm not too ridiculous for you, Harper. I'm determined to learn everything there is to know about you, so I can't go scaring you off before I've done that."

She scoffs. "Why would you want to know anything about me? I'm just a small-town—"

"There is nothing 'just' about you, June. Trust me."

She studies me for a long time after that, like she's trying to dig beneath the surface and get to the good stuff. I know the feeling; it's the same way I'm looking at her. "What do you want to know?" she finally asks. "Your assistant already got all the details."

"Dex got town gossip. I want to know the real June."

Color brightens her cheeks, and I praise the fact that it's not freezing outside because it means I can try to extend this walk as long as possible. I meant what I said, and I want to know as much as I can about this woman while I'm still in town.

"Tell me about where you grew up," I say.

Giving me a sidelong glance, June fights her smile but gives in when she sees mine. "I had a pretty normal childhood, though maybe a farm boy like you doesn't know what that would be like."

"You're right. I spent my childhood milking cows and collecting eggs at the crack of dawn. Did you grow up in Denver?"

We walk and talk for over an hour, comparing city life to farm life. June tells me about how she was an only child, which is so different from my family of five kids, of which I am the youngest. She talks about being a high achiever and going to law school because her parents wanted a good life for her, but now they have started bemoaning the fact that they raised a career-oriented woman and haven't gotten any grandkids yet. June gets quieter when she mentions that part, and I honestly can't tell if she wants a family or if she's happy running her store in this small town.

To take the attention off of her, I tell her about how my siblings are all married and settled, living respectably quiet lives within forty miles of where we grew up in Idaho, so my parents are happy with their horde of grandkids. Although, it doesn't stop my mom from wondering when I'll move back home and add to the chaos despite being at the height of my career right now.

"How did you end up in Hollywood?" June asks.

I make eye contact with an older couple sitting on their porch even though there's not much to see this late at night and it's on the chilly side for porch sitting. We've passed them twice already, and I'm pretty sure their glares get stronger every time. I don't answer June's question until we're out of earshot, though I don't have any good reasons to be suspicious. Sure, they kept their eyes on us the whole time we walked past, but they're probably just nosy neighbors.

I glance back at Richie to see if he's noticed them too, and his scowl is pretty telling. At least it's not just me being paranoid, though I can't decide if that's a good thing. What is up with this town?

I clear my throat and force myself to pay attention to my beautiful date. I can't remember the last time I met someone this easy to talk to, which is saying a lot because I've never struggled for conversation. I hope it's not only me who feels a connection here. "It may come as a shock to you, June, but I have a flair for the dramatic."

June snorts out a laugh and leans into me. "What? You? I never would have guessed!"

Yes, give me all the sarcasm. Her willingness to joke around with me means she's warming up to me, and nothing could make me happier. "It's crazy, I know. My parents thought it was a good idea to throw me into every community production they could because they didn't know what to do with me otherwise. An agent came across a video of me someone posted online when I was seventeen. She got me my first gig in LA, and the rest is history." I chuckle. "Pretty much everything about my life after that is online, so I might as well stop talking now."

"I like when you talk." June's steps falter as she blushes again. "I mean you're fun to talk to. Obviously, since talking is your job. I just mean you're...not as annoying as I thought you would be." She grimaces, making me laugh.

"Wow, coming in hot with the compliments."

She joins my laughter, shaking her head at me. "I'm saying you've surprised me, Jonah James. Not many people are interested in knowing much about me. And I don't remember the last time someone got me to talk this much. Especially a man."

"Do you talk to men often?" That's a stupid question. She runs a hardware store, which is the average man's playground. But I don't like the idea of her being surrounded by men who would notice how attractive she is. Was I one of many to take an interest in her after stepping through her door?

June rolls her eyes. "No, I tend to avoid men. But something about you has piqued my curiosity."

I laugh, though this feels too close to most people's reasons for inter-acting with me. Most people don't care who I am, just that I'm famous. "I know, I know. These good looks are impossible to resist."

"No," she says without hesitation. "It's more than that. It's something about *you*. You're genuine and easy to talk to."

Oh, she's playing with fire now by saying nice things, and I pull her to a stop so I can look her in the eyes. And by eyes I mean mouth because I'm a simple man, and a compliment like that makes me want to kiss her 'til the cows come home. Huh. Apparently talking about home has pulled the farm-speak out of me. "I could talk to you all night, June Harper."

She lifts her chin, which feels a lot like an invitation. "Is that so?"

I nod and lean in, my heart picking up a frantic rhythm. She's giving me all the signs, signs I couldn't ignore even if I wanted to. "I could also do other things."

June blinks slowly, her gaze slowly shifting from one of my eyes to the other. "Like what, Jonah James?"

I reach up and brush a finger along her jaw. "I could kiss you. If you'd let me." I hold my breath.

Humming, she lifts her tempting lips in a crooked smile as one of her hands grabs the front of my jacket and pulls me closer until we're practically breathing the same air. She smells incredible, drowning out the rest of my senses with the soft floral scent that envelops her. "You're asking permission?"

"I like to think I'm a gentlem—"

June rises up on her toes and presses her mouth to mine. Her lips are soft and warm and disappear far too quickly, leaving me buzzing and dizzy. She smirks, her dark eyes dancing in the glow of a nearby street light as if she knows exactly how deeply her actions affected me just now. "I've always had a thing for gentlemen," she says with a soft laugh.

I'm not sure I can form words. I hoped for a kiss, but I never expected one, and June has left me completely dumbstruck. It's ridiculous, considering I spent a good chunk of the day working with the chemistry coach on set to make sure Bonnie and I are selling our relationship in the movie. But Bonnie isn't June, and none of the on-set kisses felt like this one.

None of them left me wanting more.

"Walk me home?" June asks, and I nod dumbly.

We're quiet until we reach her house, where the mangy orange cat sits on the porch with a disgruntled expression, like he's angry that I kept June out past curfew. I glare at him—he's standing right where I'd like to give June a proper kiss—but then he pads down the steps and rubs up against my leg, purring loudly.

June shakes her head, bending down to pet the cat. He darts away from her touch and disappears into the bushes. She huffs. "I don't understand that cat."

The shift in subject knocks some sense back into me, giving me the power to speak again. "He makes perfect sense. I happen to be incredibly likable."

June matches my smile, warming the air around us by ten degrees. "I guess I can agree with him on that. Thanks for the walk tonight, Jonah. This was nice."

Nice? This was *epic*. I would walk with her every night if I could, just to hear her talk about herself. Especially if I can get a kiss out of it too. "I'm filming most of the day tomorrow, but..." My words trail off as something sparks into memory. Something I learned this afternoon but conveniently forgot until now because I was so focused on June.

Bonnie and the author—Hank—aren't really dating. Their relationship is a publicity stunt, which is a pretty normal thing in our line of work but causes problems for me because today I was enlisted as backup. If their relationship falls apart, I'm supposed to step in as Bonnie's new flame to make sure her tenuous popularity doesn't drop.

I agreed because saying yes is my default setting and I like Bonnie enough to want to help her, but I don't think I thought it through. Besides, that was before June kissed me. Before I thought I had a chance.

I clear my throat and lead June up the steps to her door, wondering if I can tell her about the Bonnie thing. It may never happen. Bonnie and Hank look pretty into each other despite their relationship being a sham. But what if it does happen? I can't date June if I'm putting on a show with Bonnie.

"But?" June pushes when I never finish my sentence.

Smiling, I tuck some hair behind her ear. "But I'll try to stop by your store if I get a chance." I hold back a wince at such noncommittal words. They make me sound like a tool, and June already has plenty of those in her life. *One problem at a time.* If I need to step in as Bonnie's fake boyfriend, I'll tell June everything. Until then, I'll continue as normal and hope for the best.

My stomach lurches, but I ignore the discomfort and press a kiss to June's forehead, lingering there and breathing in the floral smell of her hair. "Mm, I'm definitely coming to your store."

"What's your real name?" June whispers.

I can't help but laugh. "I knew you were curious."

"And?"

Pulling back, I give her my most charming smile and walk down the steps. "And you still need to earn it. We never did have ice cream." I wink, and her groan of frustration washes away my worries. Optimism will be a much better approach with all of this.

Hank and Bonnie will do fine, which means there's nothing standing between me and June Harper. I have to believe that.

I stand on the sidewalk, Richie waiting in silence a few feet away, until June goes inside and locks her door. Almost the instant she's gone, the orange cat returns to my side. This time, he has a torn piece of paper in his mouth, which he drops at my feet before head-butting me.

Curious, I bend down and pick it up, reading the words scrawled on the lined page.

If you're going to make moves on the actor, you'd better be planning to leave town with him when the movie is finished. Or else.

Or else what? Cold dread ripples through me. Handing the page to Richie, I take one step toward June's door but stop myself. It might not even be relevant to June, so why bother worrying her over nothing? Right before June turns off her porch light, I catch sight of a strip of something shiny in the middle of her door. Tape. With a scrap of paper that matches the tear on the note.

"They left that for June while we were out walking," I say in horror.

Richie grunts. "You don't know that."

"June would have said something about it if she knew. The cat must have pulled it from the door before we got here." I look down at the cat, who stares back up at me with ugly yellow eyes, like it knows exactly what it brought me.

"It's not necessarily a threat," Richie says, though he hardly sounds confident in his assessment.

"It looks like a threat to me." Now, more than ever, I'm convinced someone is trying to get rid of us. All of the set disasters, the props trailer, Bonnie getting stuck... That's one thing. Now they're going after June because she agreed to go out with me? That's not cool.

"Rich," I say, hands clenched into fists as I start heading back toward Main Street where we left the car.

"Where are you going?" He hurries to catch up to me.

I don't know. My thoughts are spinning, leaving me dizzy and disoriented. I feel like I need to jump into action and *do* something, but I don't know what to do. I hate that. But I can't sit still. I pick up my pace, nearly in a jog now.

"Jonah!" Richie grabs my arm.

I tug myself free and keep moving. "They're going after June now," I growl. "I'm going to stop them."

Grabbing me again, this time Richie holds fast so I can't escape. "You're being irrational, Jonah. Think for a second. You don't even know who's doing this."

I groan. "It's not a ghost."

"I know."

His admission seems to settle something in me so I'm less amped up, my thoughts slowing. "Oh. I thought—"

"There have been too many events targeting the movie for it to be anything but sabotage," he says with a shrug. "Sorry for losing my mind for a bit there."

That gets a tense chuckle out of me. Richie is usually the logical one, and it bothered me more than it should have that he thought it was a ghost behind all the nonsense. "Glad you're seeing the light, Rich."

He rolls his eyes. "Yeah, yeah. As for this thing with June, I'll look into it. But maybe you should reconsider—"

"They've gone too far with this. We need to figure out who it is and make them stop before someone gets hurt." Before *June* gets hurt. It's my fault that she got dragged into the mess, and guilt settles heavy in my gut. "I should have shown her the note instead of walking away," I mutter, looking at the paper in Richie's hand. We're only a block away. I could go back...

Richie grimaces. "It's late. I should get you back to your trailer. Show her tomorrow."

"But—"

"Let me do my job, J." A bit of worry enters his expression as he looks at the dark houses around us. "I don't like you being out in the open like this after everything that's been happening."

I want to argue—June deserves to know about the threat—but Richie rarely gets worried like this. Even when I slip past him to interact with fans in a crowd. He's nervous, and the last thing I want is to stress him out so bad that he quits. I wouldn't lose just a bodyguard; I'd be losing a friend.

"Okay," I murmur and reluctantly follow him the rest of the way to the car. I would much rather be back on June's doorstep to make sure nothing happens to her, but I'll listen to him this once.

"I don't like that look in your eyes," Richie warns as we climb inside. "You should stay away from her."

I narrow my eyes. "Not going to happen."

"Jonah, you're only going to be here for a few weeks."

Though it's one of his defining features, I hate when Richie gets logical. But he's right. Am I really going to get worked up over someone who can only be a temporary part of my life? Staying away from her would keep her safe, and it's not like she wanted me to pursue her in the first place.

But *she's* the one who kissed *me*. No one can claim she's indifferent.

I try to get my body to relax as Richie makes the short drive back to the production field. It's not working. I should keep my distance, but I don't know if I'll be able to.

"She kissed me, Rich," I mutter, staring out the window at the dark town.

He barks out a laugh. "I was there." *He's always there.* "And she's not the first person to do that."

Women kiss me all the time if they make it past Richie and the rest of his security team, but this was different. "There's something about her that I can't get out of my head."

"I know."

I groan. "I don't want to keep my distance."

"Even if it would keep her safe?"

"Something tells me June can take care of herself." At least, she can when she has all the facts. Grabbing my phone, I send a message to Dexter, who is more than likely still awake because I swear the man doesn't sleep.

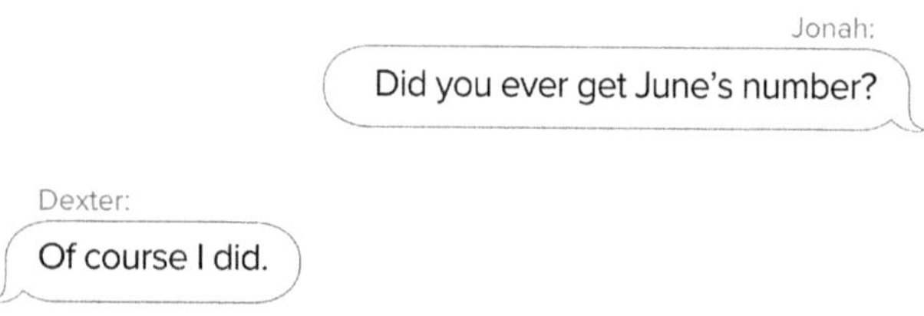

I grin when he sends the number, and I add June to my contacts before sending a text to her.

It takes ten minutes for her to respond, and by that point I'm already back in my trailer, which sends a shiver through me every time I step inside because it's smaller than I prefer. But it's not like I have anywhere else to stay, since Laketown doesn't have a hotel and the only bed and breakfast in town doesn't have locking doors because the owner doesn't believe in that kind of thing.

Yeah, I think it's weird too.

I settle on my couch and try not to fidget while I wait for June's text to come in, and when it does, I am way too quick to unlock my phone for anyone to call my scrambling dignified.

I send her a picture of the note.

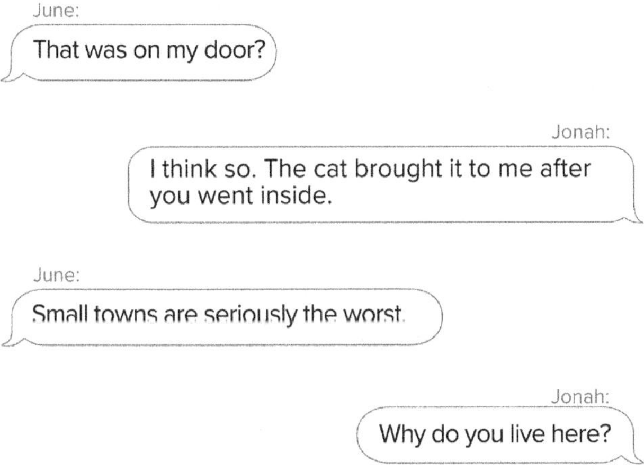

Dots pop up, telling me she's typing, but they disappear after a moment. Pop up again. Disappear. It's a full minute before her text shows up.

Once again, it takes her a long time to respond, which makes me think there's a lot more to the story than what she tells me.

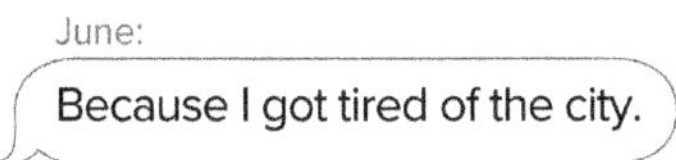

I'm tempted to ask for the real reason. I learned a lot about young June tonight, but I know very little about the woman she is now. Ignoring my curiosity, I stick to the topic at hand.

Jonah:

Your best option is to ignore me and go about your life so they don't have a reason to threaten you again.

June:

I could do that, yes.

I grin, imagining her sarcastic tone as she says that. She may not match my enthusiasm about spending time together, but she's interested. I know she is.

Jonah:

Or you could say screw it and hang out with me whenever possible, which is the option I like better.

June:

I have no idea how you make cocky look so good, Jonah James.

Jonah:

Lots of practice.

June:

I don't think I need to be worried about this, honestly. Laketownians are annoyingly tame.

Jonah:

Except when they sabotage our movie sets.

June:

Have they done that?

Jonah:

I don't have proof, but it's either that or a ghost.

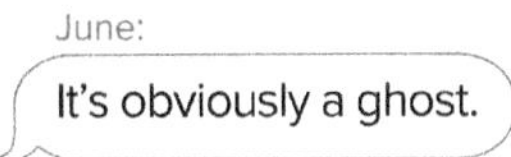

I chuckle at her dry humor and wish I could have had this conversation with her in person instead of over text, but I'd rather give Richie some peace of mind where I can. He's a permanent fixture in my life, and I need him to stay that way. But I wouldn't mind adding June to the mix, which means I need to keep trying to prove to her I'm a good guy. By some miracle I haven't messed things up so far.

The dots pop up. Disappear. Pop up again. Disappear. When she doesn't respond, I send another text and hope I didn't push things too far.

I debate for only a second before hitting the call button. I'm riding pretty high after that response, and hearing her voice would only make the night better.

"Is texting not enough for you?" June says instead of hello.

I chuckle. "I don't think anything is enough for me when it comes to you. If I come to your store tomorrow, can I kiss you?"

"You're really asking that?"

"Call me crazy, but I'm a firm believer in consent, and I'm not about to—"

"You're not crazy. I'm glad you asked." She's quiet for a moment. "My... I was engaged back in Denver, before I came here. He never asked."

Cursing under my breath, I sit up straight as my blood pounds through my ears in anger. "Did he—"

"No. Nothing like that." June sighs. "For the most part he was a decent man, but there were moments... He's the reason I left Denver. Why I don't generally trust charming men. You never know what's lurking under the veneer."

Well there goes my good mood. Again, I wish I was with her so I could...I don't know. This doesn't feel like it would be a good time to hug her, and patting her arm would be the lamest form of comfort. But I want to do *something*. Why does this town always leave me feeling helpless? "June." I swallow a thick knot of regret that sticks in my throat. "I'm sorry if I pushed you into anything. I shouldn't have—"

"Jonah James, you are far too perfect for your own good. You didn't push me into anything."

"That's debatable."

"If I didn't want to go out with you, I wouldn't have. I learned a few things from my ex, so that relationship wasn't entirely worthless."

"Do I want to know what you learned? What was his name?"

"The Ex. I don't use his name because he doesn't deserve that."

I shake my head, smiling despite myself. She is the most intriguing woman I've ever met. "You are remarkable, June Harper."

"And you owe me ice cream and a real name, Jonah James."

I laugh. "I'm getting a little too used to you calling me Jonah James, so I don't know if I want to tell you anymore. You'll be sorely disappointed. But ice cream? That I can do."

"Tomorrow?"

"Wow, *someone* sounds eager." And I wish I could say yes, but that's going to be a tough one. "I can't do tomorrow. I'll find a time to get away and give you that kiss you agreed to, if you still want it, but I'm going to be shooting until midnight, most likely."

"That sounds horrible."

"It's part of the job. Particularly when that job is a murder mystery. We haven't shot any of the night scenes yet, and Bonnie's going to be out of town next weekend for a wedding or something, so the director is trying to pack a bunch in while he can."

"Bonnie's leaving town? Is...never mind."

Chuckling, I settle back into the couch now that our conversation has strayed from her stupid ex. I stretch out and get comfortable, hoping this conversation ends up being a long one. "Her author is going with her, if that's what you're asking, though I hope you're asking something else. I'm still not convinced you aren't interested in the guy, and I want to keep that interest for myself."

"I'm not sure I like jealous Jonah James."

"Oh, you haven't seen me jealous, June Harper. It's taking all my power not to be my usual clingy self."

She laughs, and the sound is music to my ears. "There is no world in which I can imagine you being clingy."

"Is that a challenge?"

I may not be able to see her, but I'm convinced June rolls her eyes. "You are..."

"Something else?" I finish for her. "You do have a habit of telling me that. But I should know if you like clingy or not, because that's going to change how I act around you."

"Ah, see, this is why I don't like actors." But I can hear the smile in her voice, so I'm not worried. "How am I supposed to trust anything you say to me, Jonah James?"

"Because I might be falling in love with you, June Harper, and I don't have any plans to mess things up."

"You're not falling in love with me," she says, her voice thick with derision.

"No," I agree with a chuckle. "But I could."

She doesn't respond for several seconds, and her voice comes out soft. "You don't even know me."

"Now *that* is a challenge if ever I heard one." Especially now that I know she has an idiotic ex who didn't deserve her. My eyes land on the note, which I left on the table across the trailer from me. I still want to figure out who's messing up my movie—*need* is a better word—and I want—need—to spend as much time with June as I can while I'm here. Maybe I can kill two birds with one stone. "Hey, June?"

"Yeah?"

"I have an idea. How do you feel about solving a mystery?"

chapter seven

June

I don't see Jonah for three days. Not even when I try to visit the set, though I can never get close to where he is. I would be worried that I did something wrong except for the fact that he sends a million texts during the day and calls me each night, talking to me long into the morning hours even though he should be getting way more sleep than he is. The director, Beckett, has gotten paranoid and won't let anyone near his movie, and Jonah is almost desperate for a chance to get away once Bonnie and Hank head to New Mexico for the weekend.

"I thought getting locked in a trailer was bad, but this is a million times worse," he says over the phone. "Even Richie is feeling trapped, and he's one of those weirdos who likes small spaces."

I smile as I sit on my porch with a pinch of tuna, trying to coax Samson out of the bushes. I don't know why I even try, when he hasn't shown any signs of warming up to me. I guess I'm feeling weirdly lonely. Probably because Hank has been spending all his time with Bonnie, and he's the one person in town I ever talk to.

That's not true. I've talked to a lot of people around town the last few days, trying to get any hints at who might be sabotaging the movie set, with no luck. What a waste of limited small talk energy.

"I don't know if I would call an entire field a small space," I tell Jonah.

"It is when you have several hundred people all trapped together. And even with all of Beckett's precautions, we still ended up with a busted water tank this afternoon."

Samson pokes his head out of the leaves, nose working hard, but his eyes are locked on mine, and he seems to be saying, *I won't fall for your tricks.*

I toss the tuna onto the sidewalk and roll my eyes when the cat darts out to grab it before returning to his hiding spot. "Did no one see who did it?"

"You can't see ghosts, June Harper. That's the problem."

I laugh. "Okay, but you said I could help you figure out who's causing all these problems, and so far I am missing out on all your promises. The chance to solve a mystery, ice cream..."

"Making out with a super hot movie star?" Jonah adds.

Heat flushes through me, and I'm so glad he can't see me right now. We video chatted last night, but I didn't want him to see my pitiful attempts at buying Samson's love tonight, so I stuck to a phone call. "Making out?" I repeat. "Jonah James, that is quite a leap from a simple kiss."

"There is nothing simple about the way you kiss."

I am so glad he can't see me blushing. "Bonnie's leaving tomorrow, right?"

My question makes him laugh, though maybe that's because my voice came out strained. I would *love* to make out with Jonah James, and somehow over the last few days he's come to know me too well for me to hide that fact. I didn't realize it was possible to get to know someone this well over the phone, but this man gets me talking in a way no one ever has. "Yes, she's leaving tomorrow, which means Beckett will be focusing on all the side character scenes and filler shots over the next few days. And that, June Harper, means you can have me all to yourself."

Every time he says my full name like that, another part of my wall crumbles. Although, I think it would have started collapsing anyway after I told him about my ex. His initial reaction was so perfect, even without knowing the things my ex did or said, and I'm pretty convinced now that I don't have anything to fear from the charming Jonah James.

I didn't think anyone would ever convince me to try dating again, but Jonah has been building up an impressive case in favor of giving him a chance while he's here.

"What's your real name?" I ask.

No matter how many times I've asked that question over the last few days, his answer has always been the same. "You gotta earn it. You know that."

At this point, I'm not sure I'll ever learn his real name. Maybe his name is actually Jonah James and he's messing with me, but I wouldn't even care.

Scooping out another chunk of tuna, I hold it toward Samson's bush and try not to think about the fact that Jonah's life is in Los Angeles while mine is in the middle of nowhere, Colorado. We are from two completely different worlds, and as soon as he finishes filming, he'll have no reason to come back here.

"You haven't had any trouble today, have you?" Jonah asks. He does this all the time, asking questions out of nowhere and changing the tone of our conversations, but I kind of love it. He is so easy to talk to, and we can go from teasing to serious and back again without any awkwardness in between.

I shake my head, forgetting I'm talking to him on the phone when Samson pokes his head out again, this time taking a step toward me. "Oh, um, no. I was at the store all day, and it was pretty dead."

A little too dead. Business is always slow in a small town like this, but the last few days have felt extra quiet. I may not make enough to cover overhead next month, but I'm not too worried. My profit margins have always been small, and I still have some money in savings to cover a bad month here and there.

The perks of winning a lawsuit after your ex trades emotional abuse for physical abuse and pushes you over your limit. In a strange way, I'm glad he was my boss. Because we were at the office, he was on camera when he hit me; I never would have had any proof otherwise, and I might not have had a way to start a new life if not for that lawsuit.

"Why did you decide to buy a hardware store?" Jonah asks.

Samson gets close enough to reach the tuna with his tongue, but as soon as my fingers twitch with excitement, he vanishes back to the bush.

I groan.

"Sorry," Jonah says. "Should I not ask about that?"

"No, it's not that. It's Samson. I nearly had him before he bolted."

Jonah laughs, and I try to picture his wide grin. It's only been a few days, but the details of his magnetic smile are already fading—seeing him on a phone screen isn't the same. I hope he's right about being able to get away from the production field tomorrow. "I wish I knew how to help you with that cat, but I'm as baffled as you are."

"Says the cat whisperer." I squint as a car turns onto my street, the headlights blinding until it makes the full turn and passes my house. I should go inside—it's after eleven and too cold to be outside—but I am determined to make some progress with this dumb cat. "Did you have any cats growing up?"

"Do barn cats count? Because they were kind of evil, so I don't know if I would call them pets. One of them bit me when I was seven, and I half expected to turn into some sort of were-cat at the next full moon."

"I still can't picture you on a farm, Jonah James."

"Then you're not thinking about me often enough, June Harper."

Geez, this guy knows how to make me blush. And it doesn't bother me in the slightest, which is a strange feeling. My ex liked to make me blush, but never in a good way. I think he liked having that kind of power over me every time he embarrassed me or called out my flaws.

"I bought the hardware store because it was available," I say.

"That's it?"

"That's it. Pretty boring, huh?"

"Nothing about you is boring. I could spend my whole life learning about you."

I'm used to honesty. Hank, the only real friend I have here in town, is always very open about what he's thinking or dealing with. Granted, it took some time for him to trust me, but I think he needed a friend as much as I did when I moved here from Denver. But despite my being accustomed to my incredibly honest friend, Jonah keeps catching me off guard when he says things like this.

He chuckles. "Did I freak you out again?"

"No," I lie. Well, it's only a partial lie. I love that he says whatever he's thinking; my reaction is the part that freaks me out. I've spent so long thinking I would live the rest of my life alone that it's hard to come to terms with trusting a guy like Jonah.

"I did freak you out," he argues. "And that's fine. We have a mystery to solve anyway, so I can't have you getting all moony-eyed every time we're together."

Scoffing, I grab one more scoop of tuna. If Samson doesn't go for this one, I'm giving up for the night. "You wish I was moony-eyed."

"I do, but I'm under no illusions that you'll fall for me overnight. I'm prepared to put in the work."

This man... "And you think solving a mystery with you will win me over?" My eyes lock on the yellow ones staring at me from the bushes. *Come on, kitty kitty.*

Jonah hums thoughtfully. "I think you miss aspects of your old job and are champing at the bit for a little excitement in your otherwise mundane life."

His response catches the breath in my throat, leaving me stunned. The tuna slips from my fingers, but I don't care. "How...?"

"Believe it or not," he says smugly, "I pay attention to what you tell me, June Harper."

"I have not told you I miss my old job. I've told you the opposite, in fact."

"You told me that you hate your boss, The Ex, which is understandable, but every time you talk about the work you did, something in you lights up."

Now I wish we *were* on a video call so I could see the expression on his face. I don't even know what to say to him. I'm in complete awe of this man who has somehow become one of the people who know me best in only a matter of days.

"Jonah James," I whisper as another car pulls onto the street.

I frown. That looks like the *same* car from earlier, its white paint scuffed and rusted in places, and it's moving way slower than it needs to. I watch it go, not liking the fact that I can't see the license plate well enough to read the number. It turns at the end of the street, like it might make a full circle of the block.

"How goes your cat project?" Jonah asks.

"Hang on a sec." Wiping my hand clean on my jeans, I move to the porch and crouch behind the bush where Samson is hiding. If anyone were to come up to the porch, they would find me, but no one should be able to see me from the road.

"Is he getting close to you?"

"Yeah," I breathe, but I'm not talking about the cat. I'm talking about the headlights that pull onto the street a moment later and slow, shining on my front door for several seconds before moving on at a glacial pace.

Heart pounding, I shift my stance so I can watch through the leaves as the car heads down the street.

It'll be back.

"Jonah," I say, keeping my voice low. "I'm going to tell you something you're not going to like."

"Have I lost my cat whisperer status?"

"I think someone is watching my house."

He curses, and his tone instantly shifts into something hard and protective. "Who is it? How do you know? Are you okay?"

"There's a car that keeps driving past the house. I don't know who it is, but I think they're waiting for something."

"Are you still outside?"

I'm afraid to say yes, but my silence seems to answer his question anyway.

"Get inside. *Now*. I'm sending Richie over."

I check to make sure the street is dark and empty, and then I dart into the house and lock the door behind me. "Why would someone case my house like this?" I mutter as I double check the locks on the back door and all the windows. "I haven't even seen you in days."

I expect a witty quip, but Jonah remains serious. "Maybe someone heard you talking to me, or me to you. Maybe it has nothing to do with me at all. Are you inside?"

I turn off the light in the front room and peek through the blinds. "Yeah. I haven't seen the car come back yet. Maybe I was being paranoid?"

"I'd rather be sure than take a chance." He says something away from the phone, his voice muffled, and I hear Richie's deep voice reply. They talk back and forth for a minute while I keep an eye on the street. "June, I think—"

"He's back." As headlights flood my yard once more, I step away from the blinds so the person in the car doesn't see me, and I feel strangely separated from my body as I stand in the middle of the room. Waiting. The last time I dealt with something like this, I was helping one of Hank's neighbors avoid a guy trying to take her kids from her. It was less terrifying when it wasn't about me, but now I'm shaking. "What should I do?"

Call the police, a voice in the back of my head says. But if I do that, I'll have to disconnect from Jonah, and that's the last thing I want.

"What's he doing?" Jonah's voice wobbles and fades, like he's moving his phone to the other ear or something.

"I don't know. The headlights are shining right on my window."

"Faster," Jonah says. Not to me.

My eyebrows pull low, and I look down at my phone in alarm. "Jonah James, tell me you are not with Richie."

"Can't tell you that."

"Jonah! You're way too valuable to—"

He barks out a bitter laugh. "I'm a farm kid from Idaho with a pretty face. Let's not pretend I'm anything special."

But he is something special. He has only known me for two weeks and only taken me on a single date, and yet he's rushing to my rescue without any idea of who or what is waiting outside my house.

"We're almost there, June," he says.

Only a few seconds later, the headlights seem to grow brighter, and then the light shifts, leaving my window. There's still light outside, like the car hasn't left, but I'm too spooked to peek out there to see what's happening. What if they don't go away?

Someone knocks on the door, scaring me out of my wits, but then Jonah says, "It's me."

I scramble to the door and tug it open, though I should have been more cautious. But at the sight of Jonah standing on my doorstep, phone to his ear, relief floods through me. Exhaling, I throw my arms around him and bury my face in his chest. He wraps me up tight, holding me in a way I've never been held before.

"You're okay," he whispers, stroking my hair as I tremble against him. "I've got you."

He *does* have me, and I feel myself start to fall apart in his arms. It's like whatever bravery I usually have slips away beneath his touch, leaving me bare and vulnerable.

"I got the plate," Richie says from the porch. "I can make some calls, but my guess is they wanted to scare her, whoever they are."

"It worked," Jonah growls. "June, we can stay here tonight if you'd like." The hard edge to his voice tells me he isn't really asking.

My instinct is to say no, to brush off the fear and look after myself like I've done my whole life. But now that I'm in Jonah's arms like this, I don't want to leave. I feel so safe. "Stay," I whisper. Then I tilt my head back and look up at him. "Will you get into trouble?"

He smiles. "Nah." We're still standing in the doorway, so he gently nudges me backward so Richie can follow us inside and lock the door behind him. The bodyguard moves to the window, but Jonah keeps his arms around me. "I've indulged Beckett's paranoia long enough, and it's not like he can kick me out of his movie for sneaking out at night. Who would he get to replace me? Derek Riley? *Please.* I'm way better looking than him."

I pull in close to his chest again, glad for once that I'm not tall. I'm relaxing now—I'm pretty sure I overreacted—but I have no desire to leave this spot. I fit so perfectly. "I don't know if you can call it paranoia. I think... I was asking questions about the things happening on set. I clearly asked the wrong thing at some point and made someone angry."

Jonah tenses. "You were asking questions?"

"As if I'd let you solve the mystery on your own. I figured I would get a head start while I waited for your prison guard to ease up." I sound braver than I feel right now.

Chuckling, Jonah returns his hand to my hair and runs his fingers through it. "I am both annoyed and impressed, June Harper. Rich, might as well run that plate. It could be a good place to start in the morning."

"Got it." Richie moves to the kitchen, already talking to someone.

Again, I think about calling the police, but I already know what the sheriff would tell me. He's as against this movie as anyone, and he would tell me I'm being paranoid and to let him know if there are any actual crimes.

He would be right. Driving past my house isn't doing anything wrong, no matter how much it freaked me out.

"You can go to bed," Jonah tells me. "Richie and I will hang out in here."

I look at my couch, which isn't all that large. It'll fit one of the guys, but barely. I hardly expect either of them to stay up all night, so where will the other one go? Besides, I doubt I'll be able to sleep knowing someone out there is vindictive enough to stalk my house. My hold tightens around Jonah as I imagine someone trying to get through my bedroom window because the locks are old and flimsy. I've been meaning to replace them all, considering my house is older than me, but I've never felt unsafe in Laketown. Not until tonight.

"Or," Jonah says softly, "I could sleep on the floor in the hallway, if that would make you more comfortable. Tell me what you want, and I'll do it."

I don't know what I want outside of the fact that I do not want to be alone tonight. Taking a deep breath, I reluctantly pull myself out of Jonah's hold and offer a sheepish smile as I run my hands over my hair. "Thank you. For coming over. I don't usually get spooked like this, so I…" My words falter when I get a good look at the concern in his eyes. He's so worried, and warmth spreads through me from my head to my toes. "Will you stay in my room?" I ask. I immediately regret being so bold and shake my head. "Forget that. I shouldn't have…"

I trail off when Jonah's fingers brush my cheek. His smile is so soft and gentle that I feel it everywhere. "Whatever you'd like, June. As long as it makes you feel safe."

In all the times I talked about my ex over the last couple of days, I didn't tell Jonah that my ex hit me. That the class ring he always wore left a small scar over my cheekbone, right where Jonah touches now. But he seems to know, and his quiet offer of protection leaves me feeling dizzy and overwhelmed.

Tears welling up in my eyes, I lean up on my toes and press a kiss to Jonah's cheek. "Thank you," I whisper and lead him to the back of my house.

Grabbing a spare blanket, I look around the small room and try not to think about the fact that my full bed might get awfully cozy.

But then Jonah takes the blanket out of my hand and lays it on the worn hardwood in front of the window seat that looks into my backyard. "Do you have an extra pillow?" he asks, like offering to sleep on a hard floor is a normal thing for a guy to do.

I furrow my brow. "I can't ask you to sleep on the floor, Jonah." And what happened to his flirty side? The one who less than half an hour ago was joking about making out with me? Not that I want to make out while I'm frazzled like this, but still.

As he sits on the blanket, legs stretched out in front of him, he looks up at me with a crooked smile and shakes his head. "If you're suggesting I share the bed with you, then you have a much higher estimation of my self-control than you should."

I can't help but smile back at him, and my body relaxes even more. The tightness in my chest eases, letting me breathe fully. I overreacted, but I'm glad he's here. "Are you saying I should be worried about your intentions, Jonah James?"

"I'm saying I haven't seen you in three days and I'm still thinking about that kiss you gave me. But I'm not one to take advantage of a traumatic situation." His eyes darken as they drop to my mouth. "No matter how much I want to."

A shiver runs through me.

Before I can say anything, Richie lumbers down the hall and stops in the doorway. "We should have a name in the morning." He raises an eyebrow at Jonah, but he doesn't say anything to him. Instead, he looks at me and asks, "Is there anything you need tonight, Miss Harper? I'll keep an eye out for any trouble, but you should be safe the rest of the night."

I haven't talked much to Jonah's bodyguard before now, but I find myself tempted to wrap him up in a tight hug. Which is ridiculous because I'm not much of a hugger, except when it comes to Jonah, apparently. Richie doesn't look like the type to appreciate a hug, but I'd be okay with giving Jonah another one as a proxy.

"Thank you, Richie," I say after a longer pause than I'd like to admit; I was imagining Jonah's arms around me again. "I think I'll be okay in the morning, but I'm woman enough to admit I wouldn't be okay if you weren't here." I look at Jonah. "Both of you."

Jonah's smile fills the room with light. "I'm not one to ignore the chance to be a knight in shining armor, June Harper. Even if my daring rescue is mostly me sleeping on the floor."

As Richie heads back to the front room, I grab a pillow and hand it to Jonah. "You don't snore, do you?" Not that I have any right to complain if he does.

Chuckling, he shakes his head and stretches out on the floor, one hand behind his head. In his t-shirt and sweats, he's showing off all his trim lines and muscles. I need to change into pajamas and brush my teeth, but I spend a moment looking at him and trying to figure out how a movie star ended up happily sprawled on my floor.

"You are not anything like I expected, Jonah James," I mutter and head for the bathroom. If I get any sleep tonight, it'll be a miracle. And not because I'm scared.

Nope, I'm going to be dreaming about Jonah James all night.

CHAPTER EIGHT

JONAH

Note to self: try not to sleep on any more floors.

When I wake, the sky is still pretty dark outside, June is sound asleep, and I feel like I got hit by a truck. I like to think I'm pretty spry for a thirty-two-year-old and used to sleeping in strange places while I'm on the road filming, but my back was not meant for hardwood. Nor was my heart meant for worrying the way I did last night. I don't think I slept much because every little noise made me think someone was coming after June.

Sitting up and stretching, I watch June for a few minutes and marvel at the way she handled things last night. She was scared, but most people would have been full-on panicked. I almost was, and I'm glad Richie agreed to come check on her. I'm more glad he gave in when I told him I was coming whether he joined me or not.

Yeah, he said whoever was in that car was probably just trying to scare June into minding her own business, but what if he was wrong? What if someone had tried to hurt her?

I run a hand through my hair and tiptoe out of the room to where Richie is propped up on the couch, eyes fixed through the open blinds to the front yard. "Anything happen last night?"

He shakes his head. "All quiet."

"Did you sleep at all?"

He doesn't have to answer that question. When he's on high alert, Richie doesn't sleep. I have no idea how he does it. I swear there have been weeks during press tours where he only gets a few hours of sleep over the course of several days, but he keeps chugging along like it's nothing.

I finally understand how he feels when he's in charge of my safety, and I don't know how he handles this kind of worry all the time. I feel like I'm one jump scare away from falling apart.

"What about the license plate?" I ask through a yawn I can't hold back. Now that the house is bright with morning sunshine, I'm relaxing. Barely.

Chuckling, Richie lifts his phone with a shrug, showing me the black screen.

I groan. "Dead? We need to get you one of those supercharged batteries or something. Or keep a portable charger in the car." Though, knowing him, he would forget to charge that too. "I'll check and see if June has a charger you can use."

It's not until I poke my head into the bedroom that I remember she's still asleep. These late night shoots have been killing me this week, and only partially because my late call times meant I couldn't talk to June until midnight or later. And I've been desperate to talk to her every day, which is ridiculous because we've been on a single date and shared one too-quick kiss that barely counts for anything.

Hasn't stopped me from reliving it.

Like a creep, I lean my shoulder against the frame of June's door, my hands in my pockets, and watch her sleep. Does she feel our connection as much as I do? Sure, she hugged me like no tomorrow last night, but

I'm giving all credit to the actual creep in the car. If she hadn't been spooked, I wouldn't have gotten an embrace like that, and that's fine.

But now that I've gotten a taste of what it's like to hold her, I want to do it again.

June looks a lot less fierce when she's asleep. Of course she does. But her dark hair is a mess around her head, and her mouth hangs open slightly as she breathes deeply, like she doesn't have a care in the world now that someone is here to look out for her.

I *want* to take care of her. To make sure she has no reason to feel any fear in her own home. It took her a long time to fall asleep last night—I spent that time listening to her toss and turn and telling myself that it was a bad idea to start up a middle-of-the-night conversation—and she's probably exhausted from her ordeal last night. But what can I actually do to help her?

I only have a couple of days' break while Bonnie is out, and I plan to spend as much time with June as I can. But I don't want to pressure her into solving this sabotage mystery with me. She's been talking a big game the last couple of days, but that was before things got personal. I wouldn't blame her for wanting to step back, though that would make it harder for me to enjoy her company.

My mind needs to figure out who's trying to ruin our movie. My heart needs...

I swallow, biting my tongue as June stirs. My heart wants her. It wants to know if this is more than a simple attraction. And if it is? That's going to raise a lot more questions I won't have answers for. I'm a Hollywood actor from LA who rarely has breaks in his schedule. She's a business owner from a small town in Colorado and seems content to stay that way. There's no way this can work.

But I don't know if the reality of the situation is going to stop me from trying.

June opens her eyes and finds me in the doorway, and the smile that lifts the corner of her lips heats a ball of lead that has been in my chest since our kiss. If that thing goes molten, I may never cool down when it comes to this woman, because everything she does seems to add a little heat.

"You're still here," she says, her voice scratchy.

I fold my arms. "What kind of guy do you take me for?"

"The kind who has better things to do than hang around here."

"Agree to disagree. I can't think of anywhere better."

Her blush heats the ball inside me another few degrees, as I knew it would. "Jonah James," she whispers and runs a hand through her hair to smooth it.

Time to change the subject before my exhaustion convinces me boundaries are for suckers. "Do you have a phone charger Richie can use?"

"What kind?"

"USB-C. I already know you don't have an iPhone."

She rolls her eyes and reaches behind her side table. "Are you an Apple purist?"

Her teasing question eases some of the tension still lingering from last night, and I breathe more easily knowing she isn't completely traumatized. "Me? No. But Dexter is, and he's the one who buys everything for me. I suggested an Android once, and he broke into tears."

Chuckling, she sits back up with a black cord in hand. She looks at it for a second and shudders before holding it out to me.

I frown. "What?"

"Nothing." But then she grins. "Hank put something in the book he's working on. Gabrielle almost gets strangled by a phone charger."

Grimacing, I gingerly take the cord from her, like it might spring to life and try to end me. "That's gruesome. Are we sure Bonnie's safe with this guy?"

"Technically it was my idea to use the phone cord."

"Ah, so *you're* the gruesome one. Got it. Remind me not to get on your bad side. Or the author's."

Wrapping herself in a blanket, she follows me out of the bedroom looking adorable. More than ever, I want to wrap her back up in my arms and feel like I'm good for more than pretending to be someone I'm not. When I held her last night, I felt truly useful for the first time in a long time.

"I don't think Hank has a bad side," June says.

I snort a laugh. "The guy who writes murder stories?" Turning to look at her as I walk, I tilt my head and make a face of disbelief. "Not sure I believe you on that one. And for the record, he's one of the few people in the world who don't like me, which says more about him than it does about me."

She whacks my arm with a hand that's still gripping her blanket. "Hey, Hank is a good guy. It's not his fault you were playing his character wrong."

After handing off the charger to Richie, I press a hand over my heart and cluck my tongue. "June Harper, you wound me. I was following the script."

"You didn't think to read the book before you started filming the movie?"

I don't want to lose June's smile or her teasing, but that's inevitable with what I'm about to say. If we're to have a shot at something, I might as well be honest with her. "I would have if I wasn't in Idaho right up until I had to fly out here to start shooting. My mom has been sick."

Her smile falters. "Oh. Is she okay now?"

"I hope so, but it's hard to say. She's old. I'm the baby of five kids, remember?" Seventy-one isn't *that* old, but it's up there.

"I think she still has a lot of time left," Richie says, giving me a sympathetic smile.

June looks at him, tilting her head to the side. "You've met her?"

"Many times."

"Richie has been with me a long time," I say, counting back to when he first started working with me. "Eight years?" He nods to confirm. "He's basically part of the family at this point, and my mom knits him a sweater every Christmas."

The longing look June gives me is enough to make me weak in the knees. It's like she has never heard of anything better than a woman making a sweater for her son's bodyguard. "I love that," she says softly. "I always wanted to learn how to knit, but my mom never had time for that kind of stuff, so she never taught me. To be honest, I never had the time either until I moved here. The curse of being a career woman, I suppose."

I told her last night that I think she misses her old job. With the way her expression turns wistful and distant, I stand by my assessment. "I don't see anything wrong with having a career," I say. "Some women knit. Some women put people in jail."

She laughs. "For the record, I was never the one prosecuting. I saved that for my ex." My fingers curl into fists at the mention of him, something June notices. Pulling her lips between her teeth, she fights what I'm going to assume is laughter and says, "Is this Jealous Jonah coming out again?"

"I have no reason to envy your ex." My growly tone would say otherwise, but whatever.

"So you're feeling...protective?" She tilts her head as if confused by the idea.

Was she not here last night? "I feel absurdly protective over you," I admit with a sigh. "It's kind of awful, especially if you're going to be courting danger."

She snorts and adjusts her blanket more securely around her shoulders. "I'm not courting danger."

"But last night—"

"We overreacted. This is Laketown, and no one would be stupid enough to do anything dangerous."

I'm not sure I agree with her, but she's far more relaxed than she was last night. If she's not worried, maybe I don't need to be either. Ha! Fat chance of that. The rising heat in my chest is proof that I might be worried about June for the rest of my life.

Still looking like she might laugh, June smiles at me and says, "Can I make you two breakfast to say thank you for coming over last night? It's not nearly enough, but I—"

"It's plenty," I say, rubbing my chest as if that might soothe the building pressure. "Thank you. But let me know if your eggs turn out to be empty so I know if we're dealing with a ghost."

As I expected, June's eyebrows drop low, and her words are hesitant. "What do you mean, empty?"

I am as serious as I can be when I reply, "Exactly as it sounds. The set ghost took a whole pallet of eggs and left hollow, intact shells. The head of catering almost called an exorcist."

"That's...strange."

"You're telling me." It's the one thing I haven't been able to justify as a human act so far, but I'm trying not to think about it. It's easier to swallow if I crack jokes about it. "Can I help you with breakfast?"

Before June can respond, Richie barks out a laugh and says, "Better say no, Miss Harper. He's terrible in the kitchen."

"Hey!" I complain. "How am I supposed to impress this woman if you tell her things like that?"

To my delight, June leans up and kisses my cheek, her blanket-tucked hands wrapped around my bicep. "I think your ego is big enough, Jonah James. I've got breakfast. You can hang out here."

I watch her head back down the hall to the bathroom, and then I point a finger at my bodyguard. "I mean it, Rich. You'd better not ruin this for me."

Smirking, he shakes his head and speaks quietly as he turns his phone on. "I don't think trying to impress her will do you any favors."

He's right. June wasn't impressed by me at the beginning, and the more things I admit to her, the less she likely thinks of me. She's too smart and self-assured to take me at surface level, which is something I haven't experienced in a long time.

"It's intoxicating," I murmur, touching the spot on my cheek where she kissed. "The way she makes me work for it."

"It's been a while since you even cared."

Harsh as that sounds, he's right. I don't remember the last time I wanted to try with a woman. Or anyone, for that matter. If it hasn't been relevant to my job, it hasn't been my priority. My lack of dates lately was as much my own fault as it was a shortage of genuine options.

"Are you going to survive the effort?" Richie asks.

"Shut up." But I match his smile before dropping onto the couch and resting my head on the back, eyes closed. I'm so tired. I'm hoping June has coffee. If not, I'm more than happy to stop by the little shop in town, even if the young barista squeals whenever I step inside. Or maybe I should get Dexter to bring the coffee to us. Then I wouldn't have to move. That sounds nice.

Richie elbows me in the ribs, and I open my eyes to find June standing in front of me with an egg in her hand. The house smells of bacon and toast, and it's a lot lighter than it was a second ago. How long was I asleep?

"You lied," June says, raising an eyebrow.

I run a hand down my face, regretting the way my neck was cricked back. "About what?"

"You do snore."

A smile cracks my lips. Stretching my neck from side to side, I search for some witty retort but come up blank. However long I was asleep just now, it wasn't enough. It's a good thing I'm not filming today, or makeup would have their hands full making me look like less of a zombie than I feel.

"Is that my breakfast?" I ask, nodding to the egg in June's hand. "Generally, eggs are better when they're out of the—" June sets the egg in my hand, and I freeze, dread rolling through me. "It's empty."

Am I about to start believing in ghosts?

June snickers. "You should see your face. Look closer."

I do, though I have to blink a sleepy film out of my eyes before I notice the tiny holes on either end of the egg.

"People blow the contents out of eggs sometimes to paint them," June says as I hand the egg to Richie to examine. "It's not easy, especially with holes that small, but it can be done. And I'd bet if you looked at the eggs that the catering staff had, they would have holes like these."

"That's a strange prank to play," I mutter, wishing I had taken the time to look at the cursed eggs rather than accepting the catering staff's story point-blank. But why would I have done that?

June shrugs. "But did it work? Seems like it had some of you spooked."

"*I* wasn't spooked," I say. Totally lying. "But yeah, some of the crew are still convinced it was a supernatural occurrence. So this could be proof that there is someone out there trying to get us to leave. The question is who?"

"Phil Collins," Richie says.

His tone is so matter-of-fact that I wonder if my mouth and brain aren't connecting and I asked something different. "What?"

"The car last night. It belongs to Phil Collins." Again, nothing about the way he says it suggests this is a strange joke he's trying to tell; Richie is notoriously giggly when he tells jokes.

I rub my face again, marginally convinced I'm still asleep. "Are you telling me June's stalker last night was a British rock singer?"

When June pats the top of my head, I feel extra baffled as she says, "It's a good thing you're cute, Jonah James. Phil Collins lives here in

Laketown." Then she heads back into the kitchen as if that's a totally normal thing to reveal.

I jump to my feet to follow her. "One, I'm not going to forget that you think I'm cute. And two, I'm pretty sure Phil Collins doesn't live in small-town Colorado. Last I heard, he was in Florida or something."

Grabbing a frying pan of eggs from the stove and moving it to the table, June takes her time arranging the breakfast spread she's made us. When she finally turns to look at me, her eyes are dancing with amusement. "Phil was born and raised here in Laketown and has never left. Obviously Richie didn't mean the drummer from Genesis." She gestures for me to sit and smirks.

As Richie takes the seat next to me, I glare at him. "You could have told me that part sooner."

He shrugs. "Hey, I only got a name. This looks great, Miss Harper."

Richie and I wait until June has served herself before we dig in, both of us taking far less of the bacon and eggs than we would if we were at catering. If we were home in Idaho, Dad would have made double the amount that June did for the two of us, but he also would have overcooked most of it. When Mom first got sick last year, my dad took on cooking duty, but he's still getting the hang of things. Half the time, one of my sisters heads over to the farmhouse to make a bunch of freezer meals, and I've been considering hiring a chef for them so Dad can focus on the farm.

He's long past retiring age, but he'll only stop working the land when he's dead. Even then, he might try to make it happen. He's still spry and hearty, but I don't know how long that will last.

I make another mental note to get in touch with my agent. I'll need to be in as many movies as possible next year if I'm going to pay for a personal chef on top of everything else I secretly do for my parents.

"You look pensive," June says, pulling my attention away from my plate. How long has she been watching me? "Are you still stuck on Phil Collins?"

I chuckle, wrinkling my nose at her. "While I'm disappointed that I won't get to meet one of my music idols, my thoughts are elsewhere. But I appreciate your concern."

"Idols, huh? Phil Collins?"

"It was the soundtrack to that Disney movie, *Tarzan*, that did it for me."

June snorts out a laugh. "I never know what to think of you, Jonah James."

I need to find a way to fix that. I don't want her to always be guessing when she could simply take me as I am. "How can I change that?" I ask, reaching across the table to grab her hand.

Her eyebrows fly high, but she doesn't pull her hand away. I'll take that as a win. "Not sure," she says. "Right now, I'm more focused on the fact that Phil tried to scare me last night. I don't know the guy much outside of what I already told you, other than his sister also lives in town with a couple of kids, but he lives on his own. I don't think he left the note the other night because he's notorious for his atrocious handwriting."

"And I don't think he could have been the one to lock us in the props trailer," I say, nibbling on a piece of toast and trying not to stare at the remaining eggs. June's cooking is far better than catering's. (In their defense, the catering staff is cooking for an entire film crew, and my nutritionist has kept my meal options pretty limited.) "It was decidedly a woman's voice we heard."

"You are aware people can disguise their voices, right?" June says with a smirk. "I thought you of all people would know that."

"Maybe, but I have a sense for these things, and it was definitely a woman."

Hopping from her chair, June searches through a drawer before returning with a pad of paper and a pen. Before she sits, she picks up the pan of eggs and dumps the rest on my plate. "I can make more if you need it."

I always need it. My protein-heavy diet keeps me looking the way I should during filming, though I think my trainer would faint if she saw how much fat I've eaten this morning between the eggs and the bacon.

"I'll be good," I say instead of requesting more. "Thanks." I offer some of the eggs to Richie, but he gestures for me to eat. He's too good to me. "What are we writing down?"

As she settles back in her chair, June starts writing as she talks, which is insanely impressive. "We need to figure out who's messing with your movie."

"Because now they're coming after you?"

She looks up, one eyebrow raised and her lips pursed together. "Because they're starting to bug me. People in this town can complain all they want, but I don't like the way they're forgetting there are good people on the other side of this. So we're getting to the bottom of this."

The attorney side of her is coming out in full force, and I can't help but grin. "Are you sure you want to do this, June? Last night—"

"Last night was annoying and made things personal. We're solving this, Jonah."

"Yes, ma'am." And dang if her forcefulness isn't wildly attractive.

"There have been instances both in town during filming and on the field where the crew is set up. The tire, Bonnie's harness, the eggs and water tank..."

"And about a million other things," I add with a roll of my eyes.

June chuckles as she writes down several of the instances. Dexter must have told her about some of them, because I certainly didn't. "Add the note left on my door," she says, "and Phil driving past my house over and over, and we have a lot of instances to connect. We have at least three different suspects, unless the woman who locked you in your trailer also left the note. I'm guessing they made a copy of the trailer key somehow, but that's circumstantial at best, and it won't be easy to prove."

I study the columns she makes, frowning at the lack of evidence we have. "That's a whole lot of nothing," I murmur, thinking hard about any other details we might have. "The crane operators said it was something with the wiring, so we might want to look into anyone who has electric training."

June purses her lips, then writes down a few names. "If I knew my neighbors better, I could add more people to this list, but I'm not all that friendly with my fellow Laketownians."

"Why's that?" And why would anyone in this town decline a chance to be best friends with this woman? June is fantastic. She's interesting, independent, bold, beautiful... There must not be any single guys in this town, or they would have set their sights on her immediately.

Shrugging, June sets her pen on the table and keeps her eyes on the paper in front of her. "I guess I didn't want to lay down any roots."

That shouldn't make me feel hopeful. It means she probably feels untethered and wayward—exactly how I've felt for the last decade and a half—but it also means she might be willing to leave Laketown. It means there's a chance, however small, she would consider moving closer to me and making a go of this thing between us.

Let's not get ahead of ourselves, Jonah. She doesn't even know your real name.

I clear my throat and shovel the last of the eggs into my mouth. "We need to talk to people in town to get some answers," I say with my mouth still full. *Classy.*

June frowns, and I hope it's because of what she says and not because I'm a brute. "I tried that, remember? And it got Phil stalking my house."

"Is Phil going to be an actual danger?" I ask, glancing between Richie and June. I don't know if I can take another night like last night.

June shakes her head at the same time Richie shrugs. "He's like a hundred pounds soaking wet," she says, "so I could take him, but he's also incredibly timid. Either someone put him up to it, or someone borrowed his car."

"Which means we have even less information," I grumble. "And talking to people is the only way we're going to get answers."

"But—"

"We're going to need to go undercover."

June stares at me like I've grown two heads, which isn't exactly bolstering. "Undercover? You know this is a small town, right? Pretty sure everyone knows what we look like."

"What do you think undercover means? And have you forgotten that I'm here to film a movie?" I stand, grabbing all three of our plates and bringing them to the sink. I may not cook, but I am a master dish washer. Grabbing the sponge and some soap, I clean while I talk. "We have a whole makeup department, and some of them are incredibly good at what they do. They could make us look like completely different people if given a few hours to work their magic."

"A few hours?" June is suddenly at my side, snatching a soapy plate from my hands before I drop it in surprise at her nearness. She rinses the plate and grabs a towel to dry it. "Is this going to be a whole day affair?"

If I have any say in the matter? Yes. "As long as you're okay with that. I know you have a store to run."

"The store will be fine if I don't open today." Her shoulder brushes mine as she reaches for the next plate. Then brushes again. And then we're standing side by side, arms pressed together, and I am perfectly content with this situation. "I'll admit," she says, "I wasn't thrilled about the movie being filmed here, but that doesn't mean I want you to leave."

She means 'you' as in the film crew collectively. Deep down, I know that. But I'd much prefer she means 'you' as in 'me' and doesn't want me specifically to leave. I'll have to leave eventually, but that doesn't mean this thing between us has to end when I go. We can make this work.

Somehow.

"So what do you say?" I murmur, leaning into her and lowering my nose closer to hers. "Want to put on a disguise and be my partner in crime for a day?"

"I'd prefer to skip the crime part, but..." She holds out a wet hand. "Yes. I'd like that, Jonah James."

I take her hand and pull her in so I can kiss her cheek. I'd like to do more, but Richie is sitting right there watching us, and I spend too much of my life kissing with an audience. "It's a date," I say and smile, loving the way June blushes red as a response.

My thoughts may have gotten ahead of things, but I'm determined to catch up to them in reality. June is something special, and I'd like to keep her.

CHAPTER NINE

JUNE

I ADMIT I WAS skeptical, but Jonah wasn't exaggerating when he said the makeup team is good at what they do. As I sit in a tent and stare at the unfamiliar face looking back at me in the mirror, I'm starting to think this might work. If I had friends in town, they would probably recognize me, but I don't think any of my few casual acquaintances would know it's me beneath the wrinkles and curly gray hair.

"I'm impressed," I tell Katie as she makes a couple last-minute adjustments to my face.

She scoffs. "Of course you are." Either she doesn't like me, or she's mad the other makeup artist got to work with Jonah. Maybe it's both. "Don't touch your face," she says, squinting at me. "And don't make out with Jonah under any circumstances."

Yeah, she definitely doesn't like me.

"What if we have to create a distraction?" I ask, poking a bear I shouldn't poke.

Katie narrows her eyes. "Break a vase."

"Is that my sweetheart I see?" a croaky voice says behind me, pulling my attention to the old man hobbling inside. "My eyes aren't what they used to be." His eyes are the same golden brown eyes that stared at me so intently while we tag-teamed the dishes this morning. If not for my certainty that no one else could have the same spark in his gaze, I wouldn't recognize Jonah.

Seriously, are these makeup artists magicians? Not only has Jonah been aged up several decades, but he's also mostly bald, his bare head full of age spots. He stands slightly stooped, dressed in a colorful sweater and khaki slacks above scuffed white tennis shoes that look well loved. Even his hands holding the cane look old.

I can't stop staring.

Jonah holds a hand to his ear. "Did you say something, dear?"

"Hi," I breathe. "You look like you have one foot in the grave." I don't look as old as he does, though my floral muumuu certainly makes me *feel* old.

"What can I say? I like younger women." But then he leans close and mock whispers, "That's not true. I'm into older gals."

Blushing, I slip on the thin glasses that the costume design team left for me and get to my feet, doing my best to act the way I look. "You are a shameless flirt, Jonah James."

He cracks up and stands straight, and it's like his body suddenly reacquires all the muscle hiding under that sweater. Without stooping, he won't be able to hide his fit physique. "Okay," he says in his regular, clear voice, "we're going to have to work on your acting skills before we hit the town. My three-year-old niece is better at playing a granny."

I roll my eyes. "Believe it or not, I generally like to be honest."

He presses a hand to his heart. "Are you calling me a liar?"

"That's your entire job description."

"Fair enough." He twists his lips, studying me with a thoughtful look in his eyes. "You've read McAllister's book, right?"

I raise an eyebrow. Where's he going with this? "I've read all his books."

"Okay, overachiever." He smirks at me, wrinkles twisting with his smile. "So you know how the character I'm playing, Logan, turns out to be in on the plot all along, and it's easy to see looking back on it but not while you're in the thick of the book for the first time?"

I shrug, not sure what this has to do with pretending to be old. Also, does this mean he *has* read Hank's book? More than once? When filming started, he hadn't even read the whole script, though he did offer a good explanation for that when he mentioned hanging out with his sick mom. There is something wildly attractive about a man willing to put in the work. "Sure."

"He's acting the whole time, and the reason Gabrielle—and the audience—believes him is because everything he does is subtle. So you don't want to be all wobbly and wiggly." He demonstrates, hunching over his cane and shimmying his body as he steps toward me. He looks ridiculous, though I would have done that exact thing. "No, see, it's going to be smaller than that." Grinning, he adjusts his hold and takes another few shuffling steps toward me. "You have tired and unreliable limbs, so your steps are heavy and uncertain. Your arm strength isn't there so most of your support is in your back."

As he reaches me, his free hand shakily traces my jaw with a featherlight touch. A shiver runs through me, and his voice turns gruff. "You've lived a whole lifetime," he murmurs. "Done all the things you wanted to do. Made mistakes, had triumphs, suffered heartbreaking loss and experienced overwhelming joy. But deep down you're still the woman who befriends cranky cats and endures overconfident actors and makes my heart beat entirely for you whenever I'm near you."

Is this still part of the acting lesson? Because Jonah is gazing at me with so much intensity that I think I might catch fire. No matter what Katie the makeup artist does or doesn't want me to do, I'm likely to kiss this man if he doesn't blink or look away.

I don't think he'll mind.

"Ahem." Speaking of Katie... She waits until we both look at her—I forgot she was still here—and then she bats her eyes and coyly says, "Do you need anything else, Mr. James?"

Though Jonah lets out a heavy sigh, he shakes his head at Katie. He waits until she leaves before turning back to me, a sparkle in his eyes. "Hopefully she was nice to you. I try to avoid her when I can."

I shouldn't love that knowledge after the way she just flirted with him, but I do. "Are you sure it's okay that we used the production team for this?" Katie spent more than two hours making me look old, and I'm wearing one of the outfits worn by Gabrielle's elderly neighbor in the film.

Jonah chuckles. "More than okay. When I told Beckett we were going to try to stop the saboteur, he practically burst into tears and told me to use whatever I need." He offers his arm to me. "You ready? The sooner we figure out this problem, the sooner we can turn our attention to..." His eyes darken as he looks at me. "More important activities."

My goodness, this man is going to make me combust before the day is through.

"So what's our plan?" I ask as we leave the tent arm in arm. "I obviously didn't ask the right questions when I was talking to people in town before."

Jonah hums as we join several crew members heading into town for the day's filming. "I'll admit I'm a little rusty on examining witnesses, so I was hoping you'd be the expert here."

"I didn't think of it that way." And now my gears are turning, flipping the situation into trying to get the truth out of a prosecution case. I left most of the court proceedings to others, but often I was the one coming up with the right questions.

"We should work on our backstory," Jonah says. "I'd say we've been married for..." He looks at me, head tilted to the side. "Sixty years?"

I scoff. "Was I a child bride or something? I don't look *that* old."

"High school sweethearts. Met when you were a freshman, I was a senior." He kisses my cheek. "I spent a couple of years in Vietnam, and you dutifully waited for me."

Rolling my eyes, I point an age-spotted finger at him. "I dated all the time while you were gone, but your letters were so sweet that I couldn't bring myself to give up on you."

Jonah's eyes sparkle as he looks down at me, and he pulls me to a stop, stepping off to the side of the crew's path. "I wrote you a letter every day I was gone."

"And I kept them under my bed."

He shifts closer, taking my hand between both of his and holding it against his chest. "I carried your picture in my breast pocket."

I can't help but move in closer, mesmerized by his warm eyes and the thought of someone carrying my picture with him like that. "I...uh..." I swallow and try again. "I turned down Bobby Fleming's proposal only a week before you got home."

He gasps and pulls me flush against his solid body. "His what?"

"His proposal!" I'm overheating again, but I refuse to look away from Jonah's intense gaze. "I'm a catch, and so was Bobby Fleming."

"I hate Bobby Fleming." Jonah leans in, lips brushing mine in the barest of touches.

"Jonah?" Dexter's voice is dissonant and overly loud. Or maybe I'm just annoyed by the interruption. "Wow, they did a good job on you two."

There's no sign of irritation in Jonah's eyes, but he does look like he might laugh as he pulls away to look at his assistant. "Did you need something, Dex?"

Turning red, Dexter hunches his shoulders and shakes his head. "Well, yes. Sort of. Richie wants me to trail you guys since you won't let him come with you into town."

I furrow my brow. "Won't people recognize you as Jonah's assistant?" That's why we're making Richie keep his distance, much to his irritation. But the man's too big to disguise.

Dexter shrugs. "I'll stay out of the way."

"I don't think we have a choice," Jonah murmurs before I can keep arguing. "Occupational hazard—I'm never alone."

I don't know how much I love that aspect of his life. Doesn't he ever want some privacy? It would drive me crazy to always have someone watching me. It's why I barely kissed him on our first date, knowing Richie was only a few steps behind.

Jonah's gaze grows heavy as he glances between Dexter and me, and I can't help but wonder if he knows what I'm thinking about. "Okay, here's the plan," he says, clapping his hands together. "Dex, you're going to stay as far as you can while still keeping us in your line of sight so you can appease Richie. June, you and I are going to have that first date I promised you at the diner; it'll be a great chance to charm people into talking to us and giving us some leads."

Frowning, I try to imagine interacting with people from town without being recognized. I'm no actor, and makeup can only go so far. "What if I can't do that?"

Jonah lifts an eyebrow. "What if you can't talk to people? I think we both know you're more than capable of holding a conversation."

"What if I can't be charming?"

"Again, I don't think that will be a problem."

He has a lot more faith in me than I have in myself. "I think…" I scratch my arm, wishing I had a fraction of Jonah's confidence. "I think I should let you do most of the talking, no matter what. I don't want to mess things up when this was your idea."

That gets a chuckle out of him. "One, we should never trust my ideas to be solid because I'm not as smart as I pretend to be. And two, no matter how this goes, my main goal is to enjoy my time with you. If we catch a saboteur, all the better, but I'm not hiding my primary motivator for all of this." He leans down and kisses my gray wig. "I'm in this because you're in this, June Harper."

How in the world is this man still single? Offering a grateful smile, I lift my hand and gently pat his wrinkled cheek. "And here I thought you were trying to be selfless and save the rest of the crew from the terror of Laketown."

He snorts. "I have never been accused of being selfless."

Maybe not, but the man slept on my floor last night to keep me from being afraid. I think he is seriously downplaying his good heart, and the more I learn about him, the less certain I am that our interactions are harmless flirting. As I look up into his eyes, meeting his smile with my own, I can't help but wonder what it might be like to date a guy like Jonah James. He lives in LA, which isn't exactly nearby, but surely he gets breaks in between movies and can go wherever he wants. With the way he's looking at me so intently, I have to wonder if he's thinking something similar.

Would he come visit me in Laketown during his breaks?

Dexter clears his throat, pulling us apart. "Sorry," he mutters. "Just thought maybe you'd want to get started at some point."

"Right." Jonah drops my hand and nods. "We need code names."

Shoving my fantasies down deep, I revert back to the sarcasm that has served me well so far when it comes to Jonah. "Aww, but Jonah and June sound so cute together."

"I'm not going to argue," he says with a smirk, "but if we're going to get information, we don't want to raise suspicion."

"We could use your real name," I suggest, snickering when Dexter takes a step closer in interest.

Jonah notices too and shakes his head, still grinning. "Nah, you still haven't earned that one. I'm feeling like a Cecil."

"Cecil," I repeat, testing the name on my tongue. "What's your last name, Cecil?"

"Whatever yours is, Delilah."

"Delilah?"

He nods with mock seriousness. "Cecil and Delilah. Has a nice ring to it, don't you think?"

"I don't, actually." I take a step back so I can get a better look at the man in front of me. Jonah James has such a strong presence most of the time, but in his old man getup, he's so much softer. I don't think he can ever be without that confident glint in his eyes, though, so he needs a name that reflects those two sides of him. Soft but strong. "I think you're a Harlowe."

Jonah folds his arms. "Do you? Then what's your name, my darling wife?"

I haven't gotten that far, but now he's looking at me with feigned impatience—at least I think it's feigned—and putting me under pressure. "Um. Midge."

He raises an eyebrow. "Harlowe and Midge?"

I groan. "Okay, that's way worse than the names you came up with. Why is this so hard?"

Humming, he trails his eyes over me for a second, then looks over at Dexter. "What if I use my middle name?"

I perk up. "Really? You'll tell me your middle name?"

"If you tell me yours."

That might work, and I am almost desperate for even a part of Jonah's real name. "Deal."

"You first."

I shake my head. "It was your idea, Jonah James. What's your middle name?"

His smile shifts into something softer as he holds out his hand for a handshake. "Martin."

Taking his hand, I let the name wash over me before I say, "Margaret."

Jonah's eyes sparkle. "Martin and Maggie. I like it. And our last name?"

Much as I like the idea of coming up with something fun, we might as well keep things as simple as we can. "Smith."

Something like surprise flickers across Jonah's face, lifting his eyebrows. "Smith? Really?"

"Let's not complicate things."

"Yes, ma'am. Mr. and Mrs. Smith, reporting for duty." He salutes Dexter and offers his arm to me once more, directing me toward town.

Neither of us says anything as we make our approach, Dexter several paces behind us, but I sense a shift between us. As soon as we're within sight of town, we're going to have to pretend to be a long-married couple. Jonah told me how to act old, but I don't think his quick little lesson is going to help me act in love.

Then again, as I look over and meet Jonah's gaze as Laketown comes into sight, a burst of warmth rushes through me, leaving me with a burning sensation in my chest. It's like sitting in front of a crackling fire in the dead of winter. Warm, peaceful, perfect.

Maybe being Jonah's wife won't be as difficult as I fear.

CHAPTER TEN

JONAH

JUNE MARGARET HARPER IS, without a doubt, the worst kind of distraction, something I am reminded of when we get to the diner. I struggle with the door, pretending it's heavy, and hold it open for June, who waits for me on the other side so I can take her arm once more. We slowly make our way through the crowded room, and I help June into a booth seat like it's a daunting task for us both.

It's when June looks up at me when she gets settled, her eyes big and soft, that I forget myself and lean down, pressing my mouth to hers. It's just a peck. Less than the kiss she gave me on our walk. But I feel it down to my bones and can barely remember what I'm supposed to be doing. The ball of lead inside me burns hotter than ever.

June's hand finds my chest, holding me at bay before I move in for another, more intentional kiss, and she gives me a gentle shove to force me upright again. "Easy, tiger," she whispers. "You shouldn't get frisky in public."

I can't stop the laugh that crackles out of me. "Frisky?" Her word choice is enough to push me back into character, so I take my time shuffling to the other side of the booth and dropping into the seat without grace. I place my cane on the far end of the table and then drop my chin onto my hand so I can smile at my beautiful wife.

And she *is* beautiful. Even all oldified, June is stunning, and since the moment I first saw her after Katie worked her magic, I haven't been able to stop imagining my future life. It's been so long since I dated that I can't remember the last time I even pictured myself with another person, but I can see it now.

Not necessarily with June. I'm not that crazy. But I can picture myself old and weary, sitting with my wife on a wraparound porch that overlooks a few acres of land. My parents like to sit on the porch swing my dad built years ago and watch the sky change from dusk to dark, and they say it never gets old, spending those quiet hours together. The older I get, the more I want something like what they have.

It's never been all that accessible since my rise to fame, but maybe…

"You look ridiculous grinning at me like that," June says, her voice husky and deep in a way that pierces me straight in the chest.

My head slips from my hand. "That's your old woman voice?" I whisper, a measure of panic in my words.

She frowns. "What's wrong with it?"

What's wrong is the shiver of desire that ran through me at the sound of it. Not exactly giving me sweet old lady vibes. I shift in my seat, glad I can't easily lean across the table to kiss her again because I might never stop if I did. I cough and look around for a server before I get any ideas. I meet Dexter's gaze for half a second as he takes a seat at the bar, but I keep my focus elsewhere. "Maybe try a different voice," I murmur, catching the attention of a woman in a white apron.

"Hiya!" the server says as she comes up to our table with two glasses of water. "Welcome to Gigi's! My name is Karina, and I'll be taking care of you today. Can I get any other drinks for you two?"

I look at June, wishing I knew her drink preferences so I could better play the doting husband. My mind flashes back to this morning in her kitchen, and I smile as I remember seeing a large canister tucked away on her countertop. "My lovely wife would like a hot chocolate," I say in a croaky voice. "Coffee for me, please." I already downed an energy drink before Shara from makeup got started on my face, but I'm all for more pep in my step.

"Oh," June says, her voice less sexy and more raspy, "honey, are you sure you want the caffeine this late in the day?"

I lift an eyebrow. "Well, I was thinking—"

"You know your stomach doesn't take kindly to it after ten."

Holding back a laugh, I reach across the table and pat her hand. "You're quite right, my dear. Maybe a hot chocolate for me too then."

"You got it," Karina says, handing us a couple of menus before disappearing through a door on the other side of the diner.

"You're no fun," I say immediately, flicking open the menu to see if there's anything remotely healthy I can order. I should stick to comfort food to fit my old man persona, but my gut won't love that on top of the hot chocolate after my heavy breakfast this morning. "I was looking forward to that coffee."

June chuckles as she lifts her own menu. "I think you're plenty energetic already, *darling*. I'm not sure your old body can handle it the way it used to."

"Ah, sometimes I miss the days when you didn't have such a hold over me, Maggie dear." I can't see it beneath the makeup, but I imagine June blushing, and I can't help but smirk at her.

Narrowing her eyes, she sips her water and says, "That was never, dear."

"You're right. I've always found you the most captivating woman I've ever known."

"Well," a feminine voice says behind me, "aren't you two the cutest?"

This is why we're here—to talk to people in town—but I'm still annoyed by the interruption. I take my time turning, using my whole torso rather than my neck so I come across as stiff and inflexible. "Why, thank you," I say, flashing a smile at the middle-aged woman sitting behind me. "My wife brings all the cute. I'm just a bonus."

Snickering, the woman looks at June, but only for a moment. That's good; the less chance there is of June being recognized, the better. "Are you two new in town?"

"Passing through. We're driving across the country as a last hurrah before I die."

"Will you stop saying that?" June says, and a rush of delight passes through me knowing she's playing along. "You are perfectly healthy, Martin."

I wink at her before turning back to our neighbor. "She keeps me young."

The woman *awws* and pats my shoulder. "Hopefully you live for a long time yet. What made you stop in our little town?"

She couldn't have set me up better if she'd tried. "Oh," I say, tugging on my ear, "we had a bit of electrical trouble last night, and we found that nice RV park on the edge of town."

The woman frowns, confused, but I can see when she realizes what I mean because her gaze turns stormy. "Oh, that's not an RV park. It's a movie company."

"Movie?" June asks, her voice full of curiosity. "How exciting!"

"Maybe for some people. For most of us it's an inconvenience. They've kind of taken over Laketown."

We really haven't, and everyone has done their best to stay out of the way as much as possible. Plus, the town is getting a whole lot of money for letting us film here. Since I can't say that, I offer a frown of commiseration. "That must be frustrating. Everyone we talked to this morning was very nice."

"Actors are good at pretending," the woman grumbles. "So while at any other time I would recommend spending some time in Laketown, it's better if you steer clear and come back another day."

I nod, pretending to take her advice to heart. "We can do that once we figure out what's wrong with our rig. Is there a good electrician in town? I did some electrical work back in the day, but I'm afraid this old noggin doesn't remember things as well as it used to." I tap my head and smile.

She nods and grabs a napkin and pen. "You'll want to talk to Glen Davis. He is a magician with electrical."

As our neighbor writes down the information we need, I raise an eyebrow at June, who narrows her eyes. She seems to agree that Glen sounds like the kind of person who could tamper with a mechanical lift and strand our lead actress in the air. I didn't pay enough attention to her notes at breakfast, but I'm going to guess Glen's name is on the list of suspects.

Taking the napkin, I stretch my hand over the booth bench and shake the woman's hand. "Thank you so much, Miss..."

"I'm Stacy. Hopefully Glen can get you all fixed up, and then maybe we'll see you in Laketown another time?"

"Absolutely," June says emphatically.

Stacy gathers her things and leaves right as Karina returns with our hot chocolates. "You two ready to order?" the server asks brightly.

I'm ready to talk to Glen and figure out if he put Bonnie in danger, but I smile and order a chicken fried steak. This is a slow game we're playing, and I remind myself that the longer it takes to find the truth, the more time I get to spend with June. I should enjoy this while I can.

June orders a BLT, and when Karina asks if she wants a side salad or fries, I can practically see her gears churning as she debates her options, glancing at me as she does.

"She wants the fries," I say, biting back a smile. "My Maggie likes to pretend she doesn't enjoy potatoes more than anything."

Though June narrows her eyes slightly, her shoulders dip in what I'm hoping is relief. "Yes," she says, handing her menu to Karina. "The fries would be lovely."

"You got it." Karina winks at me as she takes my menu, and then she heads for the kitchen.

The instant we're alone, June shakes her head at me and mouths, "Jonah James."

I take a sip of my hot chocolate to hide my smirk. "I've always admired the way you eat like you're human, my dear."

And I do admire that. Hollywood is full of women who focus more on their appearance than living life to its fullest. Most of the time it isn't their fault—society forces them into a level of perfection few people can achieve without sacrificing things they shouldn't have to—but I think that's one of the reasons I'm so drawn to June. She's outside of my world where appearance is everything.

She seems like the kind of person who cares about who a person is more than what he looks like. I already know she finds me physically attractive, but I'm still curious about her opinion of the rest of me.

"Besides," I add, "you know how I feel about potatoes. The world's greatest vegetable."

"Idaho." June rolls her eyes. "Of course. Are potatoes actually a vegetable?"

"Technically, yes. Some people think it should be reclassified as a grain, but I'm of the opinion that potatoes are and always will be vegetables." Not to mention my family's farm is sustained by potato sales, and a reclassification could disrupt the status quo. Maybe it would force my dad to retire, which would be a good thing if he accepted it, but he would just work harder to keep things going.

My brother texted me while I was in makeup and said something about a drainage issue in one of Dad's fields. He asked if I could send over some money so he can pay someone to get it fixed before Dad tries fixing it himself, and I'm worried that that means Dad is losing stamina with Mom being incapacitated. Not to mention he's nearly seventy-five. He can only keep going for so long.

There must be some sort of worried expression on my face because June reaches across the table and wraps her hand over mine. "Everything okay?"

Her question shouldn't startle me, but it does. Maybe because it's been a long time since anyone but Richie asked me that. "Fine," I say out of reflex, but I frown as I look down at our aged hands and shift so our fingers are tangled together. "Maybe fine." I lower my voice so no one overhears us. "I hate being as far from my family as I am."

"Do you ever think about moving back?"

"Sometimes." But I love my job, and I can't imagine doing anything else. Mostly because I don't have the skills for anything else. Eager to find a different topic of conversation, I put on a smile and tilt my head to one side. "How many kids do we have?"

Pursing her lips, she looks like she might reject my change of subject. But after a moment, she matches my smile and says, "That memory of yours, Martin. We have three, remember?"

"Ah, yes, I always forget about that middle one. She's trouble."

"The real troublemaker is the youngest. He takes after you a little too much."

"Which is why he's my favorite."

She smacks my arm. "You're not supposed to have a favorite child!"

"Oh, but you and I both know everyone secretly has a favorite. Yours is our oldest daughter, obviously."

"Why is that obvious?"

"Because she gave you a respite from me and my inescapable need to love on you."

A laugh bursts out of June, though she stifles it as several people look our way. Dexter is one of those, raising an eyebrow when I meet his gaze and giving me an impatient look. He seems to think we're wasting our time chatting with each other, but what does he expect us to do?

"You are incorrigible," June mutters, sipping her hot chocolate and shaking her head at me.

I'm already holding her hand, but it doesn't feel like enough. So I slide my foot forward until it taps against hers. She taps back. "Only when it comes to you, love," I mutter.

"You two are darling," Karina says, pausing at our booth with someone else's food in her hands. "How long have you been together?"

"Married sixty-four years," I say proudly. My eyes stray to June's hand in mine, her fingers distinctly empty. I should have seen if the costume department had any rings, but it's too late now. "It's a miracle my Margaret has put up with me this long."

Karina smiles at the pair of us, then continues on her way.

"This is so weird not being recognized," June whispers. "I get food here all the time."

"I'm thoroughly enjoying this anonymity," I whisper back. I don't know if I could live my whole life like this, though. I've gotten used to the attention my career brings, and I'm not quite ready to fade into obscurity. Does that make me vain? Maybe. But I've always been a spotlight kind of guy, and I love nothing more than seeing the way my performances affect an audience. Make them feel something.

If I took on fewer jobs, I could spend some of my time in a place like Idaho, but cutting back on projects sounds about as appealing as telling Dexter my real name. Fewer projects would mean less money, which would make it harder to ensure my parents are taken care of. I'm no Derek Riley, who gets cast in movies without even trying, and every job I get is a relief.

"Maybe I should have let you order a coffee," June says, squeezing my hand and pulling me out of my thoughts. She's looking at me like I've been lost in thought longer than I realized.

I return her squeeze and lean closer. "You were right, and I would have regretted it."

"You didn't get much sleep last night." There's something in her expression that is so compelling, like she's trying to say so much more than her words.

I lift one side of my mouth in a smile. "Worth it."

June shifts forward, closing the distance between us. "I'm glad you were with me. I would have been terrified."

"Did you get visited by the ghost last night?" Karina asks.

I nearly let slip a swear as I sit back, startled, and remember to stay in character. "You scared me, Karina," I say with a breathy laugh and press a shaky hand to my heart. "My eyesight must be worse than I thought—I didn't see you coming!"

She winces and places our food in front of us. "I'm so sorry."

"What did you say about a ghost?" June asks. "And don't you worry; Martin scares so easily it's a wonder he hasn't had a dozen heart attacks."

I snort. "It's because my heart belongs to you, Margaret dear. You will always keep it safe for me."

Glancing between us and worrying her lip between her teeth, Karina seems to debate answering June's question, as if it might scare me again. But we *need* her to answer it.

"I do love a good ghost story," I say, picking up my utensils and throwing a smile up at Karina. "Small towns always have one."

"Oh, well..." Karina shrugs. "No one fully knows what to make of it, but there have been strange things happening around that movie set in town. It's nothing, really."

I cut into my steak, hoping that puts her at ease. "What sort of strange things? I was once convinced we had a ghost in our attic, but Margaret assures me it was a raccoon."

"There is no such thing as ghosts," June says, rolling her eyes. "I have told you this so many times."

"Normally I would agree with you," Karina says, "but no one can explain this one."

I meet June's gaze, forcing my expression to remain neutral. She isn't as skilled at hiding her skepticism, so I speak to pull Karina's attention back to me. "The whole town believes it's a ghost? You have me intrigued, Miss Karina. What has it done?"

"Oh, it's—"

"Karina!" Someone deeper in the diner waves at her and holds up a mug.

"If you'll excuse me," Karina says, offering a quick smile, "I should get back to work. Let me know if you need anything, okay?"

Once she's gone, June's shoulders slump. "That was disappointing."

"That was interesting," I argue, taking a bite of my food. It's delicious but a far cry from my strict diet. If I weren't in the middle of filming, I wouldn't care as much, but I'm likely to start craving mashed potatoes and gravy now.

More than usual, anyway.

We eat the rest of our meal in silence. I can tell June is thinking hard, probably wondering like I am if Karina was telling the truth about no one having an explanation for the disasters happening on set. If other people are like Karina and nonplussed, that could help us narrow down suspects.

When Karina comes with our bill, I pay with cash and leave a much smaller tip than I normally would, trying to come across as average. I make sure Dexter knows we're leaving, and then I struggle to stand and help June out of her seat. Maybe we'll get some answers when we find Glen the electrician, but something tells me we're far from solving this thing.

But if it means I get to spend time with June, I don't even care.

CHAPTER ELEVEN

JUNE

I'VE ONLY BEEN IN Glen's garage office once, when I first bought my store and realized the wiring was all sorts of wonky. It's been a couple of years since then, but I'm pretty sure everything looks just as it did back then, down to Glen himself and the mug of coffee sitting in front of him. The grizzled man, somewhere in his fifties, sits hunched over a paper planner, muttering to himself as he compares a couple different dates.

Jonah glances at me, holding my arm as we stand in the doorway. "Does he keep track of his appointments on paper?" he whispers, his eyes wide.

I nod. "A lot of people in Laketown are old school."

"I would miss so many meetings and auditions if Dexter didn't put everything into my phone for me."

"You're hopeless, Jonah James."

Glen still hasn't noticed us, so I clear my throat. He looks up, surprised, and takes us in. "Well hello. What can I do for you?"

Jonah nudges me, his mouth clamped shut. He told me on the walk over that he doesn't know enough about electric work to ask the right questions, so I get to handle this round of questioning.

I'm not sure I know enough either, but I'll do my best. "Good afternoon," I say, my voice as creaky from nerves as it is from trying to sound old. "We were told you could help us with a little problem we're having."

Glen's eyes jump between us. "Oh? What sort of problem?"

We should have done some research before coming over here. I don't even know how to get the conversation on the right track. "We have an RV, and the..." Shoot, I don't even know what problems an RV might have, and the way Glen is staring at me is only making my nerves worse. "The sunroof. It won't open."

Jonah snorts a little laugh, covering it with a cough. "And the lights won't turn on," he adds. Oh, that's way better. "Everything else seems to be in working order, so I think maybe there is a connection issue somewhere."

For a guy who claims to know nothing about electrical, he sounds incredibly confident, and I envy that so much. Yeah, okay, he's spent years learning to make his roles believable, but it would be a lot easier to see Jonah as a normal guy if he would stop being so perfect.

Glen tucks his pencil inside the planner and closes it, wiping his hands on his tan button-up as he stands. "I can take a look at it."

"Oh, we didn't bring it with us," I say quickly. Maybe too quickly. Jonah tightens his hold on my arm, a nudge to remind me to stay in character. I clear my throat. "We parked over near the high school, next to all those movie trailers."

Glen scoffs. "There's your problem right there."

I resist the urge to grin in triumph. "Oh?"

"The movie folk think the place is haunted."

I glance at Jonah, who shrugs minutely. "How fascinating. That woman at the diner said something like that."

Jonah chuckles, his expression a mixture of thoughtful and amused. "I thought you didn't believe in ghosts, my love."

Oh, he needs to stop calling me that if he wants me to stay focused. It's bad enough that we haven't stopped touching each other since sitting down at the diner, and the more he calls me his love, the more I might start to believe it.

Tearing my eyes from his, I focus back on Glen. "Martin is right, and I don't believe in ghosts. But if I did, could a ghost do something to our wiring?"

He snorts. "Of course not."

"What was that young man saying about a mechanical failure on the set the other day?" Jonah asks me, squishing his face into a look of consternation. "Maybe our problem is related to that."

"Something about a forklift," I reply, hoping the incorrect machine will make me sound less suspicious.

"Crane," Glen grunts. "An actress got stuck in a harness in the air for a while."

I gasp, covering my mouth in horror. "Oh no! How horrible."

Glen blows a bit of dust from a shelf next to him, looking wildly uncomfortable. "She was fine."

"What was the cause?"

"I, uh, can't figure out how the wire got damaged to the point of breaking in two. I inspected everything myself before they rented the machine, and it was all perfect. Got the movie people pretty spooked."

"So a *ghost* chewed through the wire?" I ask, unable to hide my skepticism. He's nervous about the whole situation, and my instincts are telling me to keep pushing. He knows something he's not saying. "Maybe you missed a—"

"It was perfect before I turned it over to them," he says again, narrowing his eyes at me. "Did you want to get your lights fixed, or what? I have to make a house call, and my schedule is pretty full, but my daughter just got out of class at the high school and could take a look if you're in a hurry."

"Oh." I tilt my head, trying to imagine a teenage girl fixing an RV. An RV that doesn't exist. "Oh, we wouldn't want to bother her. We're in no rush."

Glen grunts. "I can tell you some things to look for until I have a chance to get over there." His gaze turns stormy. "Could be a few days though."

"Any direction you could give us would be lovely," I say, though I don't mean it. Jonah makes conversation look so easy when he does it, and I'm annoyed that I've already messed things up with Glen by pushing too hard. Maybe I should have let Jonah handle the investigation on his own—I've clearly lost my touch.

"Do you have any tools?" Glen asks, shuffling back to his desk. "If not, you can try the hardware store on Main Street."

I perk up. "That store looks delightful."

"Sure. I hear she might not have opened the door yet today, so you might be out of luck if you need something."

"She?" I smile wide. "How inspiring to know there are women out there redefining gender norms." I squeak when Jonah elbows me in the ribs, keeping my eyes on Glen even though he's looking at me warily. "Anyway, we would love advice on where to look for problems on our RV."

"Okay, so, you'll want to check the—"

"Could you write it down?" I say as an idea sparks out of nowhere. If nothing else, we can compare his handwriting to the note that was left on my door. "Please. Neither of us can claim a good memory anymore."

Sighing, Glen looks between us before grabbing a scrap of paper and scribbling some notes on it.

Jonah leans down, burying his face in my wig as he whispers, "You are brilliant."

I feel that praise in a shiver that travels from my head to my toes. Or maybe I feel *him*. I've been trying not to relive the kiss he gave me in the diner, but I have been failing miserably because I've shared two kisses with this man now, and the only thing they have accomplished is making me want more. More than a simple peck. More often. *More.*

"You smell good," Jonah murmurs, using our clasped arms to pull me closer. "My darling wife."

Another shiver prompts me to lean into him and soak up his warmth. "It's the hairspray." My hair is plastered to my head under the wig, held down by a tight length of fabric. "I'm pretty sure I'm incredibly flammable right now."

Jonah's laugh seems to escape out of him against his will, and we both look over at Glen, who has stopped writing and is standing there staring at us. "We are on a third honeymoon," Jonah says brightly. "A last hurrah before—"

"Don't you dare say 'before I die,'" I snap, pinching his side. It's as much to stay in character as it is because I didn't like it when he said it the first time either. Jonah James is a bright spot in the world and will hopefully be around for a long time.

Glen hums and scoots around his desk to hand the paper to Jonah. The handwriting is vastly different from the note left on my door last week. "These are your basic problem areas," he explains, offering up some details for a couple of the bullet points while both of us pretend to listen intently. "And you might want to think about moving your vehicle to the other side of town."

"Is the film crew dangerous?" I ask. The alarm in my voice is only half fake.

Grunting, Glen picks up a worn leather bag and hefts it over his shoulder. "Not necessarily, but something is angry with them. Person or ghost, it would be better for you to keep your distance until someone figures out what's causing all the problems."

He shows us outside and offers a ride back to Main Street, but Jonah declines, telling Glen that we are content to walk and enjoy the sights of the town. Once Glen has driven off in his truck, we are finally alone for the first time all morning.

Or, mostly alone. Jonah's eyes flit across the street, where Dexter has found a seat against a tree in front of a house and looks all too conspicuous typing something on his phone.

"I don't think he understands lying low," I mutter.

Jonah snickers. "He's doing his best."

I can't help but wonder if Jonah ever gets tired of someone always being around. He may not be top tier in Hollywood, but he is famous enough that he brings his bodyguard home with him. Is he ever alone? That must be suffocating.

I need to change the subject before I start imagining being a part of that life, always under scrutiny. "What did you think of Glen's take on the sabotage?"

"I think..." Jonah leans in again, pulling the same move as before by burying his face in my fake hair as his arms wrap around me. "You were on to something and spooked him. Seriously, you smell so good."

If anyone smells good, it's him, and I tuck myself into his embrace. Even with Dexter keeping an eye on us, it might be time to explore that whole *more kisses* idea. I don't know when we might get another chance until we shed our old folk personas later today.

Before I can suggest ducking behind a tree and out of sight of Dexter, Jonah pulls away and grabs his phone from his pocket, reading something with a furrowed brow. "Interesting..."

It had better be interesting. "Care to share?"

"Richie says there was a sighting of someone sneaking around set about twenty minutes ago, but no one was able to get more than a glimpse because they kept disappearing; everyone who saw the person seems to have seen something different."

I narrow one eye. "Does that make it more or less likely to be a ghost?"

Chuckling, Jonah pockets his phone and holds out his arm to me. Apparently it's time for us to continue our investigation. "Honestly? I'm not sure. It could mean we're looking for more than one person."

"But that's not necessarily new information."

"And we haven't narrowed anything down yet," Jonah adds.

"Except I think we can cross Glen's name off the very long list of potential suspects."

"Really?"

I nod, sorting through my thoughts even though I can feel Jonah's eyes on me as we slowly make our way down the sidewalk. If I look at him, I'll lose my train of thought. "He was jumpy, yeah, but I get the sense that he takes too much pride in his work to let something go wrong like a broken wire."

Jonah hums thoughtfully. "But you have to admit there was something sketchy about him, right?"

"Obviously. But that's not evidence. I think we should try the grocery store next."

"Why?" Jonah turns us back toward Main Street, keeping our pace slow. "And that's not me questioning your idea, by the way. I want to follow your logic so I don't get left behind."

"I would never leave you behind, Jonah James."

"Do you promise, June Harper?" He grins at me, sending a wave of heat through my body as his eyes trace my features.

Do I mean those words? No matter how much I'm starting to like this guy, our worlds are so different that it's difficult to picture either of us being a part of the other's life. People here in Laketown seem to think he'll bring nothing but trouble—heck, I was one of those people—so I can't see Jonah settling in here very easily. And I'm not sure I could handle the spotlight of his life of fame when I have grown used to the solitude of a quiet, small-town life. It all feels...impossible.

I want to figure out who's trying to mess with the film, but there's a part of me—larger than I'm willing to admit—that hopes it takes a long time to solve this thing, just so I don't have to say goodbye to Jonah James.

CHAPTER TWELVE

JONAH

I CAN'T SAY THAT I've played anyone over the age of forty over the course of my career thus far, but I didn't think living a believably geriatric life would be this difficult. I'm blaming it on the fact that I'm not a method actor and I never have to stay in character this long. "How do old people hold their phones?" I ask under my breath, adjusting my grip for the third time since pulling my phone out of my pocket. Richie sent another text right as we got onto Main Street, and there are enough people out and about that I'm feeling self-conscious.

I was fine at the diner, but the longer I'm with June, the harder this becomes. I can barely focus on my role when she's sitting all prim and proper on a bench next to me, watching a couple of squirrels fight over a peanut.

She's adorable.

"I don't know," June murmurs, glancing at the phone in my hand. "Hold it up close and don't use your thumb to swipe?"

Doing as she suggests, I use my pointer finger to finally open the text, though it's impossible to read when it's this close to my face.

June snorts a laugh. "How's that cross-eyed look working for you?"

"It's not. Thanks for asking." Shifting the phone a little farther, I read through the text and summarize it for June, keeping my voice low. "He's pretty sure there are at least three people knocking things over and throwing pebbles, but they haven't caught any of them yet. One of them might have been on a bike because they left tracks."

Someone passes our bench, so I lock my screen and drop my phone onto my lap, as if the thing might blow my cover. Old people have phones. My mom was addicted to one of those candy puzzle games one winter and tried to get all of us to download it so we could be friends in the app. But for some reason, having a phone in my hand makes me feel young, and I need all the help focusing as I can get.

"A bike?" June asks as soon as we're relatively alone—Dexter is fully focused on a phone call right now on the other side of the street, barely paying attention to us. One of the squirrels gains control of the peanut and runs off, and June turns to face me now that her entertainment is gone. "That narrows things down a bit, but not as much as you might think. This town is small enough that plenty of people don't use their cars unless they have to."

"So, the opposite of LA," I mutter. "I'm glad we're not trying to solve a mystery back home."

"*Your* home."

Oof, I don't like how quickly she made that distinction. "Have something against big cities?" I ask, even if it's not the question I really want answered. We haven't known each other long enough for me to realistically wonder if she would consider moving to California, though I'd be lying if I said I haven't thought about it more than once since leaving the diner.

I don't know how this woman has gotten under my skin so easily, but I can't say that I'm mad about it. If anyone were to make me consider settling down, I'd want it to be someone like June. Someone on even footing with me who can match my steps and make me feel normal.

"I'm not against all cities," June says slowly. *Please say Denver is the only one you hate.* "I've never been to Los Angeles, but it looks…"

"Exciting?"

"Crowded."

Disappointment floods through me, but I hide it behind a smirk. "Maggie, darling, sometimes I wonder how you and I ended up together when we are so different." Ah, that was the wrong thing to say, and I hold my breath as several different emotions cross her face. Did I put a nail in the coffin of our potential as a couple?

She presses her lips together, eyes guarded. Taking a breath, she reaches over and grabs my hand, speaking to our clasped fingers rather than to my face. "Different isn't always a bad thing."

My breath hitches. "Some would argue different is a great thing sometimes. Different can help you grow and experience new things. Different can bring excitement to a life that seems to be severely lacking in that department."

June lets out a heavy sigh. "But different also lives far away."

Did she just say…? My heart thrums in my chest, almost painful. "Different doesn't want to think about that right now," I say and squeeze her hand.

Lifting her eyes to meet mine, she quirks her lips up in a tentative smile. "I know that feeling."

How am I supposed to concentrate on a faux ghost when I'm desperate to have a conversation with this woman and hash out our chances of making something work? Even if it's a temporary relationship, I would be all for seeing where things go. But I don't want to spook her any more than she's already been spooked, so I'm going to table this for now and try to remember that I'm playing a role right now. I'm not Jonah James.

I'm Martin Smith.

It was a bad idea to suggest using my middle name for this.

"Let's let Richie handle the ghost on wheels," I say softly, squeezing June's hand again. "You and I have a grocery date to get to."

Using my cane, I push myself to my feet, remembering my phone in my lap only when it clatters to the sidewalk in front of me. The screen lights up, revealing the picture of my family on my lockscreen.

"Oh, let me get that for you!" someone says, and panic shoots through me.

Right as a teenage kid reaches for the lit up phone, I step on it and wince when I hear the crunch. "Oh!" I say, feigning alarm. "Oh my, did I just put my foot in the wrong place again?"

"You're good at that, dear," June says, rising to stand next to me.

The poor kid who came to my aid touches my arm. "Here," he says, nudging me back a step. When he picks up the cracked phone, half of the screen is distorted. "Oh, uh, I think it might be broken."

No kidding. At least he can't see me in the picture...

"Clumsy me," I say, forcing a laugh. "That's the third phone I've broken this year."

June tucks her arm through mine, shaking her head. "I can't take you anywhere, Martin."

The teenager gives me a look of sympathy as he hands me the broken phone. "Sorry I wasn't faster."

Not only is Dexter going to kill me for breaking my phone in the middle of nowhere, but now I've gone and made this kid feel guilty when he was trying to help an old man. Stowing the phone in my pocket, I put my hand on the kid's shoulder and smile. "Oh, it wasn't your fault. Like I said, I'm the clumsy one here. Thank you."

He smiles and turns to go, but his eyes snag on June, pulling him to a stop. Frowning, he looks at her for a long moment before nodding to us both and continuing on his way.

June lets out a soft curse.

I raise my eyebrows. "Okay, wow, I wouldn't have expected a word like that from a gal like you."

"I think Herman might have recognized me," she says, her arm tightening around mine.

"Who names their kid Herman?"

She jabs her elbow into my side. "Focus! I deliver groceries to Hank every Thursday, and Herm—"

"Whoa, you do what for Hank?" She did not just say what I think she said.

June gives me an exasperated smile, and I swear her whole bearing lightens at the mention of the author's name. "I bring him his groceries."

Something heavy settles in my gut. "Can't the guy get his own groceries? He's a grown man, isn't he? Or is he one of those guys who can't do anything for himself?"

Groaning, she tugs me to an alley not far from where we were sitting. Hopefully the shadows will hide us from prying eyes, since I get the feeling I'm about to get a lecture for judging the author. "Do you seriously not like Hank?" she says, keeping her voice low. "You don't even know him."

I can't stop my nose from wrinkling. What reasons do I have to *like* the guy? "I know he's not good enough for Bonnie." *Or you.*

"That's absolutely not true."

Bonnie is basically perfect, but we can get into that later. I'm more concerned about the fact that June doesn't see my issue. "You own your own business! Why are you making deliveries for a guy who should be capable of getting his own—"

"Why are you making a big deal out of this?"

"I think you're doing too much for a guy you claim you don't have feelings—"

"He's my best friend, Jonah." June bunches her hands into fists, shaking her head as she looks up at me. "If I didn't deliver his groceries every week, he would spend his entire life without human contact, and I hate that for him because he went through something horrible before coming here and the guy needs someone who's willing to put in a little effort so he doesn't fade into oblivion. Just drop the groceries thing, okay?"

"It's not about the groceries!" I groan and go to run a hand through my hair, but I can't because there's a bald cap in the way. And this alley is smaller than I thought it was, with high walls closing in around us.

June scoffs. "Then what is it about?"

How can she not understand when she just talked about the guy like he's the best part of her life? "It's about you being sweet on Hank when he's not—"

"Not what, Jonah? And who said I was sweet on him? He's a friend!"

I gesture toward her, pressing my other hand over my racing heart. "You said! And your body language. You obviously like him."

"Of course I do!"

I groan as a sharp pain hits my chest. It's different from my usual panic, and I don't like it. I need to get out of this space. Away from this conversation. "Can we just go—"

"No, we need to talk about this." June's glare is almost as sharp as whatever is pinching my ribcage. "I *told* you Hank is a friend. That's all he is."

I huff a laugh. She wouldn't be this defensive if that was true. And if she's in love with Hank, where does that leave me? "Sure."

"If you can't trust me about this, then what else will you refuse to believe?" Her expression hardens as she stares at me. "At least now I know Jealous Jonah is kind of an ass."

"I'm not—" I cut myself off, feeling like I've been slapped in the face as soon as I process her words. *Jealous.* Cursing, I take a couple of steps toward the alley entrance, trying to breathe. Is this what jealousy—real jealousy—feels like? I hate it. "June." I can't even bring myself to look at her as reality sinks in. "I'm—"

"We should head to the grocery store before it gets too late."

I grab her arm before she passes, and she stiffens. "June, I'm sorry." When her stormy eyes jump to my hand, I let go of her arm and take a step back. It's as much to give her space as it is to gain some space for myself so I can ease some of this tension weighing down my lungs. I need to think clearly, and I can't do that when I'm stuck in a narrow alley. "I didn't mean..." What didn't I mean? I don't think any of the things I said about Hank were things I'm not feeling; I meant all of it. But I hate the way she's refusing to look up at me. Humility doesn't always come easy for me, but if ever there was a time to swallow my pride... I swear under my breath. "You were right. I'm jealous."

"Good for you." The words are icy.

I need to explain myself, but I don't know how. "It's not... I hate that he's known you longer than a couple of weeks."

June looks up, her eyebrows furrowed. "What?"

"I want that." Those three words slam into me as I speak them. I don't know if I've ever wanted anything more. "June, there's so much I want to know about you. Things he probably knows."

"Because he's my *friend*," she snaps. "Not some random guy for you to tear down because you don't like the timing of things."

"That's not..." I groan again and grip my cane with both hands, as if that might help me feel stable when it feels like the world is shifting beneath my feet. "I'm sorry. Forget what I said. It doesn't matter how you feel about Hank." That's a bald-faced lie, but if she's holding a torch for the guy, there's not much I can do. We're already from two different worlds, which makes this hard enough.

June rolls her eyes. "It feels like it matters."

"Only because I'm…" Stopping myself from finishing that sentence, I hold my breath as the realization washes over me. *Because I'm falling for you*. And I'm terrified that this woman is going to break me. I'm not the kind of guy who gets hung up on a woman. I'm married to my job, and most relationships I've been in have been casual because I can never trust my partner's true intentions.

Am I willing to risk heartbreak for a woman who may only be in my life for a few short weeks? With my parents getting older and Mom being as sick as she has been, I'm already having to prepare for loss, and I'm not sure I'm ready to face it on the romantic side of my life on top of my family. I want to trust June, I really do, but it's not that easy.

This isn't the kind of thing I can admit. Not right now. But I have to say *something*. My words come out quiet, lacking any of my usual confidence. "There's something in me telling me I can't walk away from this—" I gesture between us "—without seeing where it goes."

Clenching her jaw, June looks out at the street, watching people and cars pass with an expression I can't read. It sure isn't a happy one. "I don't know if it can go anywhere, Jonah."

Don't say that. As something in me cracks, I can't find the will to speak those words out loud.

Desperate to keep her from walking away and ending this here and now, I say the first thing that comes to mind. "What were you saying about Herman before?"

I can practically see the war behind her eyes as her lips press together and her eyebrows pull low. Part of her wants to leave, while the other is still determined to solve the stupid mystery. It's the second part that wins out. "Herman does most of the grocery deliveries," she says, her eyes falling to the ground at her feet. "And since I deliver Hank's stuff, Herman has always kind of hated me because he thinks he's missing out on a great tip."

And he might have recognized her just now, which wouldn't be good for us. Who knows who he might tell about our disguises?

"Come on," she says. "We'll have to hope Herman isn't heading to work right now because we're running out of daylight and don't have time to waste."

"It's only three."

She ignores me and starts walking down the sidewalk, her steps slow and uncertain and a weariness in the set of her shoulders. She looks the part of an old woman more than ever right now, and it's my fault.

How do I fix this?

Do I want to fix it? It's not like my life is conducive to a relationship, especially with someone far away, and I don't want to always be wondering if June is interested in another guy. Hank or otherwise. It would be easier to give up before I get hurt. Before I hurt *her* by never being around.

"Mr. Smith!" June calls. She's gotten farther than I realized and is looking back at me where I stand at the mouth of the alley. She's too far to read her expression, but her annoyance is clear in her voice. I messed things up when I talked crap about Hank, and I have two choices.

I can keep us at an emotional distance, accepting that this thing between us won't go anywhere like she said, or I can find the will to be vulnerable and admit how I really feel in the hopes that June and I can keep getting to know each other better even after I leave Colorado.

My head says the chance of a future for us is slim to none, especially after the argument we just had, but my heart? My heart is hopeful, and that's dangerous. Hope tends to lead to hurt.

"Coming, Mrs. Smith!" I call back to her, and with the way those words slide over my tongue like hot chocolate, I have a feeling my direction has already been chosen for me.

There is no world in which I want to stop calling her that, and that terrifies me.

CHAPTER THIRTEEN

JUNE

"Why did you say that?" I whisper the question to myself as I hide in the back of the grocery store while Jonah talks to the owner. Herman *is* at work, stocking jars of peanut butter near the checkout, and I thought it would be best to keep my distance. He didn't notice us walk in, thankfully, but I'm not about to blow our covers by giving him another chance to get a good look at me.

I've already made things awkward and tense with Jonah by telling him we don't have a future, so I don't want to mess anything else up.

I had hoped I'd fixed my slip up after correcting him about Los Angeles not being my home, but when Jonah started talking bad about Hank, I panicked. His reaction reminded me of my ex, whose abusive behavior began against my friends and family before it was ever directed at me.

I shiver and rub my arms, wishing I had a better place to hide than the freezer section. I really don't want to compare Jonah to my ex, but his actions earlier didn't make it easy to do otherwise. And then I went and shot down any potential we may have. I could try to fix that, but I don't know how. Or if I even should.

"I would give you my sweater," a soft voice says behind me, "but the costume department had a hard enough time hiding my excellent physique as it was." Before I can turn to face him, Jonah wraps his arms around me from behind, instantly warming me. "Is this okay?"

Another shiver runs through me, less from the cold than from the overwhelming feeling of safety I get from being back in his arms. I shouldn't feel safe after an argument like that. I should be on edge, and I am, but with Jonah's arms around me like this, all I can focus on is his sincerity and protectiveness. Last night, he stood between me and whoever was stalking my house, and I have to remember that side of him.

I lean deeper into his hold and nod. "Thank you."

We stand in silence for a moment while my anxious thoughts war with the peace settling in my heart. I thought I'd gotten through all the garbage left behind by my last relationship, and it terrifies me how quickly I got scared. What else is Jonah going to do to remind me of my ex?

No. He's not like that. I need to think about something else. "Are you done talking to Maya already?"

Jonah sighs. "No. Someone from catering came in, and I thought it would be a good idea to keep my distance." He tucks his chin over my shoulder, our cheeks nearly touching. I both love and hate his nearness. "Hopefully Maya will be so annoyed that she'll vent to us when it's our turn."

"*Your* turn." I wince, reminded of our conversation on the bench outside. "I just mean because I'm avoiding Herman. Not because I don't want to be with you when you talk to Maya." His words from the alley repeat in my mind, and I turn in his arms so I'm facing him. "Did you mean what you said?"

He wrinkles his nose and glances around, like he wants to run from my question. "You'll have to be more specific, but probably. I'm hoping you're talking about one of the good things I said and not my admission that I'm jealous of a guy who gets groceries from you." He pauses, suddenly looking nervous. "I...I want more than groceries."

"That." I swallow the nerves that bubble up inside me, focusing on the way he holds me so gently. It's like he's scared to hold me any tighter, something my ex never even considered. It helps me relax a bit more. "Do you really want to date me?"

Jonah's eyes jump to something behind me, and then he shuffles us toward the back corner, as far from the front door as we can get. When he speaks, his words are full of hesitation. It's a strange thing, coming from him, but it's endearing. "This isn't the best place for this conversation, but yes. I do want that."

My nerves double, but I think there's excitement in there too. Hiding beneath the anxiety. I haven't been on a date since leaving my ex, and I certainly haven't thought about committing to anyone. Not until Jonah. But I can't go through another argument like that one outside. "Hank is my best friend."

He groans, dropping his head. "I know."

"That's not going to change."

"I don't expect it to." He looks up again, his expression sorrowful. "I was an idiot out there."

"You were."

"But I also meant it when I said we could be something. If you want to be."

Right now, I don't know if I want that. But I want to want that. Up until twenty minutes ago, I didn't see any downsides to spending time with this man, and I hate how quickly I distrusted him. "Even if we barely know each other?"

Jonah smiles, accentuating the makeup that has transformed his face. "That's what dating is for, isn't it? I'm not saying I want forever."

My stomach does a somersault.

Whatever expression is on my face—disappointment, maybe?—it shifts Jonah's smile into a smirk, and he shifts closer, emboldened by my reaction. "I'm also not saying forever is off the table, just so we're clear. But I can't promise you anything, especially when my career is kind of riding on this Frost movie doing well."

Another somersault. "Wait, it is? But you're one of the better actors out there!"

Flinching, Jonah glances over my head again, but there must be no one close by because he relaxes, adjusting his hands so they rest clasped together at my lower back. "First of all," he says, his voice low, "I am a phenomenal actor, and you know it."

I scoff, but I'm so glad for this shift in tone. It feels like we're back to normal, even though we're not. Not until I can explain my reaction outside. "I don't know—"

"You watched *Silent Pursuit* that night when I ran past your house."

Heat splashes across my face, and I get the sudden urge to hold my head inside the ice cream freezer. He saw that? "I didn't watch... Okay, fine. I watched it."

"And?" He lifts his eyebrow, though it doesn't rise as high as it would normally. As I gaze at him, I realize his makeup is cracking, which means we don't have much more time before our disguises fail us.

I sigh. I'm not ready to get back to real life and all its drama. Can't I just stay here in Jonah's arms and joke about how he's a terrible actor when in truth he's one of the best I've seen? "And you were really good."

"Phenomenal," he repeats.

Pursing my lips, I shake my head at him but can't hold back a smile. "Phenomenal," I reluctantly agree.

"Thank you. Second of all, acting is not a stable career path unless you're someone like Derek Riley." Right. His career is apparently in danger. "I had to start on the bottom like everyone else, and it's impossible to know when I'll end up a has-been rather than a confident B-lister hoping to make it big."

His expression might be calm and chill, but there's a hint of anxiety lurking in his voice. Until our argument in the alley, I didn't know anything could ruffle this man's feathers, but maybe he's just as human as I am.

He gets jealous, and worries about his job, and says the wrong things. But he also apologizes and keeps me warm and makes me laugh. I don't want to be constantly on my guard, but I also don't know how to tell him why I panicked before. I'll just keep talking about him and hope all my fears go away.

Frowning, I reach up and gently touch his jaw, careful not to smudge anything. "That must be hard, not knowing how long you'll get to live your life the way you want."

He nods, lips pressing together. "Yeah, and this conversation isn't helping, so I'm going to change the subject." He leans into my touch slightly before pulling away and looking at the glass door next to us. "Ah, I wondered why you looked so worried when I came over, but now I understand. The dreaded ice cream you dislike so much."

I whack his arm. "I never said I didn't like it. And I looked worried because..." I guess I'm telling him now; he told me one of his fears, so it's only fair that I tell him about mine. This isn't an easy conversation for me, but if we don't have it, there won't be any point in hanging around Jonah. "I was thinking about...my ex."

"Bobby Fleming?"

I snort, grateful for the levity. "No. Bobby was delightful, and if you had died in the war, we would have had a wonderful life together. I'm talking about the other ex."

"The nameless one." Jonah makes a face of disgust. "Why were you thinking about him?" But something seems to click a second later, and his hold on me slips along with his expression. He looks horrified. Maybe even hurt. "Please tell me I didn't remind you of him."

I can't tell him that, so I keep my mouth shut.

He curses softly and takes a step away from me, like that might distance him from my ex. "Was it the stuff with Hank?"

I nod, deciding he deserves the truth. If he really wants to date me, he's going to have to know my triggers. "When I first met The Ex, he was a nice guy, full of praise and compliments. But after a while, he started making negative comments about my friends, my parents, our coworkers. Testing the waters, maybe? So by the time he talked down to me, I barely noticed it."

Without Jonah's arms around me, I'm shivering again, but he seems frozen in place, staring at me with wide eyes. "June," he mutters, shaking his head. "I would never say anything bad about you."

"But you were fine talking bad about Hank."

"I wasn't fine." He swallows and stuffs his hands into his pockets. "I hate that I judged him so quickly, and just because he's your friend and I was jealous. I've never..." He ducks his head, looking sheepish. "I've never been jealous before. And my mom would make me muck out the barn for a month if she knew the way I was talking out there."

Is it bad that I believe him? I believed my ex too when he said he loved me more than anything, so I'm not sure I can be trusted. But I *want* to believe Jonah. I want to think my dad and Hank aren't the only good men out there in the world.

I want to stop hiding from the world.

I grab my elbow and shrug. "I'm not saying my reaction was logical, I just—"

"June." Jonah reaches out, taking my hand from my arm and squeezing my fingers. "You're allowed to be wary. I'm the one in the wrong here. I'm so sorry I made you feel that way when I couldn't handle my own issues."

Letting out a huff of a laugh, I shake my head as I look up into those light brown eyes of his. He really is a good man, and I should apologize for comparing him to my ex. But the words stick in my throat, and the only thing I can do is joke. "A celebrity who takes accountability for his actions? Who knew?"

That gets a soft smile out of him, and he pulls me back into his embrace, holding me tighter than before. "We're a rare breed, I know. And I never want you to be afraid of me, June. I've been alone for a long time, so I'm bound to make mistakes as we go. Please call me out on my crap because I'm not smart enough to know when to..." His words trail off.

I look up. He's staring over the shelves toward the entrance, eyes fixed on something. "What?"

"The caterer just left. Herman was with her. Now might be our best chance to talk to Maya."

As much as I would rather keep talking to Jonah and figure out this thing between us, he's right. This could be my only chance to help with this conversation. "Let's go."

As we shuffle toward the front, keeping our steps uncertain and our arms looped together, I grab a carton of eggs. Jonah gives me a questioning look, but we're too close to the checkout now, and Maya has noticed us.

I set the eggs on the conveyor and smile, speaking before Maya can. "Are your eggs organic and free range? We only eat free range eggs."

Maya gapes at me for a moment before looking down at the eggs. "Oh. Um, maybe? We had to get these from a different supplier this week because they were a rush order."

"Oh?" I tilt my head. "Is there an egg shortage?"

Maya's face pales, fear filtering into her expression. "No, something…" She stops herself and forces a smile, glancing between me and Jonah. "I guess eggs were extra popular last week. I can contact the supplier and ask about these, if you'd like."

"That would be great," Jonah says.

Maya moves to the office directly behind the checkout, and Jonah and I share matching looks of irritation. "Why will no one talk about the ghost things?" I whisper, shaking my head. "It's like they're all terrified."

Biting his tongue, Jonah glances at the front door. "I'm starting to wonder if people actually think it's a ghost."

A shiver runs through me, definitely not from being cold. "I don't like that idea."

"Me neither, but it's not like we're any closer to figuring out an alternative."

"We need to get her to talk about it." I tap my lips, trying to think of a way to convince Maya she can trust us. We have the old person thing on our side, but if she's genuinely spooked, she'll need some persuasion.

But what can we do?

Jonah clears his throat. "Will you stop doing that?" he asks, his voice a little strangled.

I frown and look up at him, surprised to see a pained look on his face. "Doing what?"

He grabs my hand, pulling it away from my lips. "You're tempting enough as it is, Mrs. Smith."

Heat washes over me, which is a nice change from the cold dread that engulfed me earlier, and I can't stop myself from smirking at Jonah. Vulnerable conversations are important, and I'm glad he knows more about how my ex treated me, but I would so much rather spend most of our time in this lighthearted, flirty space. "What? You want to kiss me again or something?"

He groans, his eyes growing darker as he gazes at me. "You're playing dirty."

Except, I'm not playing. It's hard to believe he would be interested in me when he could have his pick of women, but I want him to be. Maybe he's not Derek Riley, but he's handsome and charming and has a smile that makes me weak in the knees. And he has a good heart, something I can't take for granted. One bad conversation shouldn't be enough to tear down all the green flags he's shown me so far.

Plus, I really do want to kiss him.

Leaning closer, I tuck my fingers into the collar of his sweater and nudge him down. "Jonah James," I whisper and close my eyes as he eagerly crosses the rest of the distance between us.

"I'm so sorry, but—oh!" Maya squeaks as we pull apart, and she looks like she wants to run away. But she's also fighting a smile. "I didn't mean to interrupt."

While I grumble nonsense words, Jonah beams at Maya and wraps his arm around my waist. His happiness has returned in full force. "We're on our third honeymoon, my darling wife and I," he explains. "Can't keep away from each other. What were you saying, miss?"

Maya's eyes jump between us before she lets her smile free. "Unfortunately, the supplier wasn't able to confirm whether the eggs came from free-range chickens, but I'm going to guess no. Usually they put that kind of thing on the package."

"Oh, I suppose we will be fine if we eat these if that's what you have," Jonah says. I'm glad he's unaffected and able to talk, because I'm still irritated that we got linterrupted. *Again.* Am I ever going to get a real kiss with Jonah? With the nature of his career, it feels unlikely unless I take up acting and star alongside him. "Do you know what this reminds me of, Mrs. Smith?"

I raise an eyebrow at him. "What, Mr. Smith?"

"That time we visited Alton and they were entirely out of sugar." He turns to Maya, which is good because I have no idea what he's talking about. "Did you know it's the most haunted place in America?"

Maya's eyes go wide. "Oh?"

"Yep. Alton, Illinois. I have a fondness for ghost stories, and everyone in town was certain a ghost had come and stolen all the sugar, when in truth it had just been misplaced by a new employee."

Oh! Now I see what he's doing, and I can't help but grin at him. "I *told* you it wasn't a ghost," I say, whacking his arm lightly. "It never is."

"She's an unbeliever," Jonah mock whispers to Maya. "Even though we keep hearing all sorts of stories here in your charming town, my Maggie refuses to think a ghost could be behind it all."

Maya chuckles, relaxing a bit as she glances between us. "To be honest, I'm with you, Maggie," she says, ringing up the eggs and putting them in a paper bag. "Most of our eggs went out on a delivery order rather than falling prey to a ghost."

"Who needs that many eggs?" I ask, hoping she'll answer.

"Couldn't tell you. It was a made-up name and a fake address."

"How do you know the name was fake?" Jonah asks.

Maya snickers and shakes her head. "Because the person who ordered them was named Brighton Early. And lived on 123 Road Lane."

Laughing, Jonah hands Maya a ten-dollar bill and pulls me tighter against his side. "I suppose I should stop believing this town is just as haunted as Alton was. How disappointing."

"Wait," I say, stopping him from grabbing the bag from Maya. "If the order was fake, where did the eggs go?"

Maya shrugs. "My employee delivered them and said they made it to the right person. They were paid for, so I didn't ask questions."

"Maybe you should have," I mutter under my breath. Out loud, I say, "I wonder if it was to that film crew we keep hearing about."

Though annoyance flashes across her face, Maya shrugs. "Maybe, but they put in their own order for eggs just a few days before that, so I don't know why they wouldn't do it the normal way. Honestly, they've given me a lot of business since they got here, and it's been kind of nice."

It's the first good thing anyone has had to say about the film crew, and I'm not sure what to do with that other than continue on the same trajectory. "I would imagine they've brought a lot of money to the town all around," I say, trying to sound thoughtful and objective.

Maya nods and hands Jonah the bag of eggs. "Not many of us like having them here, but the money is nice. I'm pretty sure it's the only reason any of us tolerate them being here."

I share a quick look with Jonah, who looks as confused as he does thoughtful. "I hope they don't cause too many problems for you," I say. "From the sound of it, they're the ones being affected by this so-called ghost the most."

Maya's eyebrows drop low, as if she hadn't considered that. But then her gaze shifts to the door. "I'm sure you'll just be disappointed by what he has to say, but if you want to ask my employee about the egg delivery, here he is now."

I flinch and hide behind Jonah when the automatic door slides open, presumably to let Herman back in.

"I think I would rather enjoy the mystery of it all," Jonah says, tucking the bagged eggs under one arm and leading me to the door. "Thank you!" He keeps himself in between Herman and me, which I appreciate, and it's not until we get a block down Main Street that he releases me.

"Are you thinking what I'm thinking?" I ask, though my thoughts have started whirling too fast for me to keep up. The egg delivery, the dangerous "accidents," the people running around the production field this afternoon...

Jonah chuckles. "Doubtful. You're way smarter than me."

"Not true. You were brilliant when you brought up that haunted town! That was amazing."

For the first time since I met him, Jonah looks completely flabbergasted, like he's not used to anyone praising him like that. He clears his throat and turns away for a moment before he returns his gaze to me. "Anyway, what are you thinking, my love?"

My love. Savoring the warmth that comes from his pet name, I try not to sound too set on my conclusion when I say, "We're not dealing with a professional."

"A professional...what, exactly?"

"Saboteur."

"Are those a real thing? Professional saboteurs?"

I whack him on the arm playfully, but my eyes catch on the sheer number of people wandering along Main Street now. School has been out for almost an hour now, and with nothing else to do, the kids tend to hang out in town before going home for dinner. There are too many of them for us to have a conversation without being overheard, and I'm starting to suspect...

"I think we might have to be done with interviews for the day," I murmur, taking hold of his hand and subtly gesturing to a group of teens wandering near us, a few with bikes and skateboards in tow.

Jonah nods and touches a finger to my chin. "Your wrinkles are starting to come off anyway."

"Thank goodness for that. I'm ready to be reasonably pretty again."

He scoffs, his eyes trailing over my face. "As if you're not as beautiful now as you were in your younger years."

"Mr. Smith, you are incorrigible."

"Actually, I can be quite corrigible with the right motivation."

I snort a laugh and tuck my arm through his so we can head back to the production field. I prefer to talk out loud if I want to make sense of my thoughts, and I'll need privacy to do that. "You are something else," I murmur, which only makes Jonah laugh. At this point, I've said that so many times that it's getting ridiculous.

The walk to the makeup tent is a slow one, but I tuck my theories in the back of my mind and let myself enjoy the peace of it, focusing on being with Jonah. Today is cool, not quite spring, and I'm content to lean into Jonah and soak up his warmth. Dexter is right behind us—he started following after we left the grocery store—but I can almost pretend that we're a regular couple out for a walk in the sunshine.

I can almost pretend that a relationship between Jonah and me might work.

"Did you learn anything?" Dexter asks once we reach Jonah's trailer.

Jonah sighs. "Not re—"

"Maybe," I say, stretching my back now that I don't have to worry about looking old. "But I need to think about it for a second and make sure I'm not grasping at straws."

"We can take you back to your house so you can shower and change." Jonah does his own stretching, raising his arms high above his head and subsequently lifting his shirt and sweater with it. I have to try exceptionally hard not to sneak a peek of what's under there, contenting myself with the memory of when he went running past my house. "Or," he continues, "you're welcome to use my trailer if you're desperate to de-age. I can use Dexter's shower."

Dexter frowns. "My shower is a tent and shared with like thirty people."

I meet Jonah's gaze, curious about how he will respond to that.

His mouth stretches into an amused smile as he reads my curiosity on my face. "You're forgetting I grew up on a farm, June Harper. I spent my summers roaming the woods with nothing but the clothes on my back and a shotgun to keep the cougars away. I can handle a tent shower."

"I can't decide if you're telling the truth," I whisper, a little horrified as I imagine this man getting attacked by a big cat. "Though, you'd probably make friends with a cougar before ever having to shoot it."

Chuckling, he throws his arms around Dexter's shoulders. "Or start dating her," he says with a wink that heats me to the core. "You know how I have a thing for older women. What do you say, June? Should we take you home, or—"

"I want to stay." I grimace when the words come out sounding desperate. *Show some dignity, June.* "I need someone to bounce my ideas off of after I've done my ruminating in the shower, and I don't want..." I stop. I don't want to revert back to the awkwardness of the alley if we're apart for too long, but I'm afraid to bring it up. Things are good between us right now, and I want it to stay that way.

Besides, there's always the chance that the saboteurs will stalk my house again tonight, and that sounds...disconcerting.

Pulling his arm free, Jonah steps closer to me and takes my hand, holding it to his chest like he did before. He clearly felt my shift in energy, with the way concern adds to the wrinkles on his forehead. "You're also welcome to take my bed tonight," he murmurs, rightly guessing some of my fears. "There's a couch in the trailer I can use, or I can see if Bonnie will let me—"

"You wouldn't mind spending a night on the couch after spending last night on the floor?"

Jonah's smile turns warm. "I wouldn't mind it in the slightest. Not if it means you'll feel safe."

Safe. Everything I didn't have with my ex. Even after the argument in the alley, I still feel safe with Jonah because he was so quick to own up to his mistakes. Sighing with relief, I lean up on my toes and press a kiss to Jonah's cheek. "Thank you."

"Dex, can you grab June's stuff from costuming? And maybe tell Richie he can stop pacing wherever he is now that we're back." Jonah waits until Dexter leaves to do as directed, and then he turns his full focus to me, eyes burning.

This might be the first time we're alone, and it looks like Jonah isn't about to waste the opportunity.

But instead of backing me up against the side of the trailer and claiming my mouth like I want him to, Jonah presses a gentle kiss to my forehead and breathes in deep. "I really am sorry about today. You deserve better than what I gave you."

I let out a slow sigh. "I'm sorry I overreacted again."

"You didn't." He kisses my forehead again. "The overreacting was all me. I'm going to do my best to make sure Jealous Jonah doesn't make an appearance again. He's awful."

For some reason, that makes me laugh, and my anxiety slips away. Maybe we'll be okay. "Were you really jealous of *Hank*? You're way more attractive than him."

"I'm not saying it was logical." He's beaming now, his eyes trailing over my face. "Do you really think I'm attractive?"

I scoff. "You're ridiculous, is what you are."

"I just need to be sure it's me and not this outfit that does it for you."

I take in his sweater and khakis, shaking my head. "I think I prefer regular Jonah, even if you make an adorable old man."

He snorts. "Keep talking like that and I may have to dress like this every day. You're welcome to anything you find in there," he says, nodding toward the trailer behind me. "Clothes, snacks, unsigned copies of Hank's books."

"Books?" My eyebrows fly high. "As in more than one?"

Chuckling, Jonah drops my hand and opens the trailer door for me. "After the first one, I obviously needed to keep reading so I could find out if Gabrielle is going to end up with Captain Stacey."

"Right?" I say that louder than I mean to, but I don't care. I'm just glad I'm not the only one shipping the two characters. "Hank won't tell

me if it's going to happen in the next book, and it's driving me crazy."
And wow, it's super attractive to hear a man saying something about
romance in a book when he could have easily brought up the many
murders in Hank's series. Hearing Jonah praise Hank's writing soothes
the lingering pain caused by his jealousy earlier, and I'm not sure I've ever
found him more attractive than I do right now. "Jonah James, you are…"

"Eager to spend the rest of the day talking to you, June Harper, but
I'd rather not do it while wearing this sweater." He smirks and holds out
his hand to help me up the steps.

Climbing inside, I take in the space that is essentially Jonah's home
during filming. I find myself smiling, even if it's not an elegant abode.
His bed is neatly made in the back, all four of Hank's books are stacked
near the sink with a bookmark tucked halfway through the third one,
and there are several pictures of Jonah's family taped to the wall.

It's all very cozy.

"I wouldn't mind getting stuck in a trailer like this," I say, grinning
back at Jonah. "Way better than the props trailer."

He narrows his eyes, his expression playful. "Let's not joke about
things like that, yeah? Although, I don't think I would have minded
getting trapped as much if you were stuck there with me. I'll be back in
a bit, okay? Seriously, help yourself to whatever."

The instant he's gone, I go straight for the drawers that hold his
clothes. Might as well take advantage of his hospitality.

CHAPTER FOURTEEN

JONAH

It takes longer than I'd like to get showered and changed, and I'm not happy about it. Richie is the first culprit, forcing me to stand by while he demands details from Dexter about our day in town. Then Beckett tries to pull me into a conversation about camera angles and closeups, even though he knows I'm terrible at that stuff. I think he's missing Bonnie and the way she constantly offers suggestions for the scenes we're filming, even if he'll never admit it. Once I finally get to the showers that the bulk of the crew use, someone figures out what I'm doing, and there's a small crowd of female staff waiting outside when I'm done. They come with a variety of excuses for why they are here, none of them very subtle.

One of them flat-out admits that she hoped I would step outside in a towel, though she and the others are thoroughly disappointed. With the number of photos that have made it to the tabloids from this field—the whole reason Bonnie and Hank are even in a publicity relationship in the first place—I wasn't about to take any chances and brought my clothes in with me.

I am so lucky that the tabloid that has been plaguing Bonnie since filming started, *Hollywood Hot Scoop*, seems more interested in her than in me, and I haven't had any stories circulate about me in a couple of weeks. The longer I can keep June away from them, the better. It's going to be hard enough to move forward with her as it is, and I can't imagine her being okay with the spotlight.

People in my career make relationships work all the time, so I just have to figure out how to keep June's private life private. More importantly, I need to figure out how to have time for her when I'm almost constantly filming. No big deal.

By the time I make it to my trailer with a couple of dinners wrapped in tinfoil, courtesy of catering, I half expect June to have given up on me and gone home. But there she is, curled up on my couch and snoring lightly. My heart twists at the sight of her so relaxed in my space, and when I realize she's wearing one of my sweatshirts, the ball of lead inside me ignites, going molten almost instantly.

I want this. With June. I want to come home after a day of work and know she'll be there waiting for me in a stolen hoodie. I want to bring her food and make her feel safe and listen to whatever ideas she has forming in her brain. I want her to give me her censure and her pride, her triumphs and her worries.

I told her last week that I was falling in love with her, and though we both knew it was a joke then, I'm not joking anymore. I really do think I'm falling. But what am I supposed to do about that? If I let myself feel for this woman, how am I going to leave her behind when filming is over? My next project is starting almost immediately after this one, and who knows what my calendar will look like after that?

I know. I know because I have movies lined up for months with a free weekend here and there but no big gaps. That's how I've always done it, and it's the only way I know to make sure I have enough money to look after the people I care about.

I groan softly, hating the ache that settles in my chest as I look at June.

There's no way this can work. But it might already be too late where my heart is concerned.

My phone buzzes, and I look at the screen even though I won't be able to read any texts that come in with my mangled screen. But it's a call, and I can see just enough to know it's my dad calling.

Leaving the dinners on the small table, I slip out of the trailer and answer the call. "Hey, Pops."

"Cinco! How's Colorado?"

I chuckle at the nickname. He's the only one who still uses it, and I love it every time he does. "Colorado is…" How do I sum it all up? "An adventure. How's Mom?"

"She was out in the garden today."

"That's amazing! But isn't it too early to plant anything?"

"You know your mother. She has to make sure the soil is good and fertilized."

I've always loved the way my mom tends to her garden as dutifully as my dad handles the potato fields. I love more that she's strong enough to be out digging in the dirt. "Do you think she's over the worst of it?" I ask, though I'm afraid of the answer. She was still pretty weak when I was there, and the doctors still haven't fully figured out what laid her low in the first place.

Dad grunts. "I hope so. I'm not ready to be without her. I don't know if I'll ever be ready."

I don't think my dad has ever said anything like that before. Not to me, anyway. I grip my phone tighter, leaning my back against my trailer. I don't especially want to talk about my mom dying after the day I've had, so I change the subject. "So what's up? How are *you* doing?" I wince as soon as the words leave my mouth. *Way to be sensitive.*

"Gettin' by, same as always. I just had a feelin'."

"About what?"

"About you. Thought you might need some advice or somethin'."

"A feeling," I repeat, rolling my eyes. My dad always has 'feelings' that are often lucky guesses.

Grunting again, Dad seems to struggle getting through the words when he says, "You don't come home as often as you used to."

No, I don't, and I don't see that changing anytime soon, especially if June gives me a chance. "You know me. Always busy with something."

"You work too hard."

"Look who's talking."

"Your mother and I worry about you."

"I'm fine."

"We worry about you getting lonely out there in California."

I snicker, thinking about the population difference between Los Angeles and the town where I grew up. "Nah, I've got Richie," I say lightly, though I know it won't make them worry any less. "And now there's..." I trail off, surprised by the knowledge that I was about to tell him about June. I've never talked about my love life with my parents, and I'm not sure I want to start now.

Unfortunately for me, Dad seems to have understood the words I didn't say, though he takes the conversation in a direction I don't expect. "You rushed off to California so quickly when you were a kid. You and I never had the...you know, *the talk.*"

I grimace. "Are you about to have the sex talk with me? Over the phone? When I'm over thirty?"

"Not *that* talk! Unless you need—"

"*No.*" Definitely not. At this point, I'm pretty sure all my bases are covered, and that is not a conversation I need to have out in the open.

With my luck, *Hollywood Hot Scoop* would show up again just for that. "What talk are you talking about?"

After a few uncomfortable grunts and coughs, Dad says, "The same one I had with your brothers and sister before they got married."

My stomach twists. "I'm not getting married."

"Not yet, maybe, but soon you'll—"

"Dad, why did you call me tonight?" I don't know why I'm nervous to hear his response, but I am.

"I told you," he says, sounding impatient now. "I had a—"

"Feeling. Right."

He sighs, like I'm making this way more complicated than I need to. I am, and I should stop interrupting him and let him talk. "You are finally startin' to understand love, aren't you?" he says.

I grip my phone tighter, which is probably a bad idea because I'm pretty sure it's barely clinging to life as it is after I stepped on it today. "That's..." I swallow and try again. "That's a bit of a jump."

"You met someone, didn't you?"

I don't think I can pretend otherwise. He would hear right through my lies. "Yeah," I say on a breath. "Yeah, I did."

"In Colorado?"

"Yep."

"She lives there in that small town you're in?"

"She does."

He whistles low, which is not reassuring. "What are the chances she'd move to Hollywood with you?"

"This is all very new. We haven't had a chance to talk about it." That's not necessarily true, but when June is the one mourning how far away I live, it doesn't inspire confidence in her willingness to join me in California. "I don't see her living in Los Angeles," I mutter.

Dad hums. "What if you—"

"Even if I got a place out here, it's not like I could spend a lot of time here. My filming schedule is—"

"More in your control than you pretend," he says sharply, cutting me off just like I did to him. "The only reason you're so busy is because you choose to be."

I sigh. "Because I have to be! I have to take every job I can get so I don't—"

"*John.*" Hearing my actual name reminds me that this man has seen me through some of my best and worst. He knew John before Jonah became famous. "I know you've been payin' for repairs around here, no matter how much you and your brothers try to be sneaky. You don't need to be givin' everything you have to other people. Your mother and I have always had plenty of our own money for that sort of thing."

But that doesn't make any sense. My entire life, my parents have done everything themselves. They practically defined frugal living.

As if reading my thoughts, Dad chuckles. "We're also both incredibly stubborn. If we can fix something ourselves, why pay someone else to do it?"

"Because you're ancient," I grumble. While I'm glad to know my parents aren't hurting for money, I can't help but think back on the many things I never had growing up because—I assumed—we couldn't afford it. "Did you not buy us anything because you wanted us to learn the value of money?" I ask warily.

Dad laughs. "Of course."

"Great."

"But I'm not here to talk about money, which you have more than enough of. I'm here to tell you that you shouldn't follow in my footsteps when it comes to love."

I choke on my own breath, completely caught off guard by this change in subject. "What is that supposed to mean? You and Mom are perfect together!"

"And it took us three years to accept that truth."

"What?" It's not often I regret leaving home only days after my high school graduation, but apparently I wasn't around long enough to get the full story of my parents' romance. "I thought you and Mom met at that rodeo and it was love at first sight."

"It was. Well no, it was *attraction* at first sight, but that's not the same thing. And while we talked and flirted and went skinny-dippin' behind the Masons' place, we didn't—"

"I'm sorry," I rasp, "when you did *what*?"

"We didn't let ourselves fall in love," he continues, ignoring my horrified question. "She was goin' back to school in the fall, and I couldn't leave my father to run the farm on his own. So we kept things casual."

"I wouldn't call swimming naked in a pond casual," I grumble, shuddering because that was not something I needed to know about my parents.

"Three summers," Dad says, pretty much monologuing now, which is strange because he's not a talker. "Three summers we wasted by pretendin' we didn't want it all. To experience everything together. And when we finally got it into our thick heads that we could have been enjoyin' married life together and makin' a family—"

"This is starting to sound like the sex talk."

"All I'm sayin'," Dad growls out, "is you can't waste time just because you aren't sure if this girl—"

"I'm sure." I switch my phone to the other hand, as if that might make those words less terrifying. But they've settled deep inside me, filling an empty space I didn't know was there until I met June. "I don't know how or why, but I think June and I were meant to be."

"Oh."

That's all he has to say? Pushing off the trailer, I start pacing as I talk. "All of that stuff about Mom, which I did not need to hear, by the way, and all you've got for me is 'oh'? I'm talking crazy right now."

"I don't think it's crazy."

"Yeah, well, you went skinny-dipping with your casual lady friend when you were in your twenties, so how much can we really trust your judgment?"

That gets a chuckle out of him, which helps me relax. A little. "John, you have never been afraid to be yourself, have you? I've always loved that about you."

I'm glad he thinks so, but can June learn to love it? "Dad," I say, slowing my steps, "I'm so afraid I'm going to scare her off. We barely know each other, and I'm heading back home in a couple of weeks."

"Did you know, they've invented these cool little devices called phones?"

"I don't appreciate the sarcasm, Pops," I grumble. "June isn't... She's independent. It's not like she'll be missing my company while I'm states away."

"Independence doesn't necessarily mean she can't get lonely."

Maybe not, but June seems pretty content as she is. I'm the one who intruded on her life and brought chaos. "I'm lucky she agreed to a date in the first place."

"Even better. You'll never have to wonder if she's interested."

That's...a good point. I stop pacing as I think about that. June isn't the type of person to get into a relationship just because she can. After all the nonsense she went through with her ex, she will only go for something she wants.

I swallow. "And what if she breaks my heart?"

"Then at least you know it works." Dad heaves a sigh. "Look, anyone who tells you love is easy hasn't truly been in love. It takes hard work and dedication, the same as anything else good in life. And what is it they say about lovin' and losin'? You can't go through life shieldin' yourself from all the bad things; you'll never know the sweetness of the good if you never taste the bitter."

As I let his advice sink in, I imagine what my life would be like going forward if I hadn't met June. I would have kept pushing forward in my career, constantly anticipating a brutal end that might never come. But even if it does—even if I stop getting cast in movies and have to take a different path—how much joy have I missed out on in the meantime by focusing on my next job instead of living in the moment?

"That's actually great advice," I mutter, though I shouldn't be surprised. Dad has always been the smartest man I know. "Though, I'm a little disappointed there wasn't a potato metaphor in there."

"The tough parts of life," he says with a chuckle, "are the boilin' water that softens you to perfection."

Oh, potatoes sound so good right now. "What are the chances Mom can send some of her mashed potatoes to Colorado? I think June would like them." And maybe I'm asking because hearing my dad's voice is making me miss home.

It was only a few weeks ago that I was there, but it feels like too long. I didn't even make it back for Christmas last year. Dad wasn't kidding when he said I don't go home as much as I used to.

"I have a better idea," Dad says. "Bring your June home with you. Your mother will want to see the woman who finally cracked open that heart of yours. Maybe June is the one, maybe she's not, but figurin' that out is the fun part. And so is skinny—"

"Please never talk about that again." Pressing a hand to my chest, I glance at the trailer behind me and smile. "Thanks for calling, Dad. I should go, but I'll keep you updated on the June situation. Good or bad. And tell Mom about her."

He chuckles. "You know I will. Good luck, John."

"Thanks."

"Does she know your name is John and not Jonah?"

My smile shifts to a grin. "Not yet."

"Maybe tell her sooner or later. She might change her mind if she finds out your name is John S—"

"Bye, Dad!" Hanging up, I take a second to breathe while I have a moment to myself. Only, when I turn my head, I find Richie standing just a few feet away, his expression hard to read in the darkness. I frown. "How much did you hear?"

With his hands in his pockets, he shrugs and steps closer. "Something about skinny-dipping and June breaking your heart. I'm assuming those two things are unrelated."

Even though I'm mortified that Richie heard my half of the conversation with my dad, I chuckle and slip my phone into my pocket. "What do you think of this whole thing?"

He wasn't with us today, but he's been there for the rest of it. He can probably see in my face just how far I've fallen for the woman asleep on my couch, and I'm curious what he'll say.

He doesn't answer for a long time, like he's trying to find the right thing to say. "You were the wildest kid when we met, J," he says slowly.

I raise an eyebrow. "I was twenty-four."

"Kid," he repeats with a smirk. "And I knew working for you was always going to be an adventure."

"Is that good or bad?" And why is my chest aching while I wait for him to answer that question?

Smiling, Richie puts his hand on my shoulder. "It's one of the reasons I took up the position. That, and your ambition was clear as day. You had places to go and things to do, and I've admired that about you."

"I get the feeling that's changing," I mutter, bracing myself.

"It's okay to slow down, John. It's okay to let someone in."

Two people calling me by my real name in a matter of minutes? I honestly can't decide if I love it or hate it. I've been Jonah James for so long, on a mission to prove myself and my talents. I love what I do, but maybe there's more to life than a successful career. Richie and my dad are two of the people I trust the most, and if they're both telling me to take a step back and reevaluate my plans...

Patting Richie's arm, I nod at him and silently make my way to the trailer door as he heads to his own.

There are still so many things about my life that are going to make a relationship difficult, but I feel a lot less stressed about it than I did twenty minutes ago. It'll suck when—if—I have to say goodbye to June, but why would I let that stop me from trying? It's not in me to give up so easily, and I can only imagine how fun a life with June could be.

How much fuller it could be with all the good, bad, and everything in between.

When I step inside my trailer, I get a split-second view of June awake and sitting upright on the couch before she throws her hands out and shouts, "Trap!"

I jump back in alarm, my head colliding with something hard. And the world goes dark.

CHAPTER FIFTEEN

JUNE

"Have I apologized yet for maybe giving you a concussion?" I bite my lip, holding my breath as I wait for Jonah to kick me out of his trailer and maybe his life.

But he chuckles, his eyes soft as he looks up at me from my lap, where he's been for the last ten minutes. "About a million times," he says, wincing when I adjust the ice I'm holding to the back of his head. "And I'm not concussed."

I'm not convinced. Ever since I accidentally scared him in my excitement and he knocked his head on a cabinet, he's been looking at me differently. Like he's not seeing me the way he did before.

I grab my phone from the pocket of my leggings, even though I have to adjust Jonah's head in the process. I'd rather not make him move, but it's not like I can use his phone instead. "I'm going to look up the symptoms of a con—"

"Would you relax?" Jonah sits up and puts his palm over my phone screen. "I only blacked out for half a second. I'm fine."

"I still think you should talk to the film nurses."

"Boyd and Gayle? They would say I have psychosis or something."

I blink. "The nurses are named Boyd and Gayle? Like boy and girl but..."

Nodding, Jonah reclines and stretches his legs out so he can rest his head on the back of the surprisingly comfortable couch. "Wait until you hear the name of the chemistry coach."

"What in the world is a chemistry coach?"

Jonah grimaces and takes the ice out of my hand, pressing it to the back of his head. "Never mind. I'm more curious about why you felt the need to shout 'It's a trap!' when I came inside."

Rolling my eyes, I settle next to him and curl my legs up on the couch beside me. Now that the adrenaline is wearing off from when Jonah hit his head and collapsed, I'm back to being completely exhausted. I didn't mean to fall asleep while I waited for him to come, and if it weren't for my worry over Jonah hitting his head, I would be so ready to fall asleep again.

"I didn't say 'It's a trap.'" I drop my voice to mimic his on that last bit. "I just said 'trap.'"

He smirks. "Fine. My question still stands."

"Technically, you didn't ask a question."

"Have you always been this lawyery, or is that the concussion talking?"

I groan. "I *told* you that you have a—"

"June. I'm kidding." Grinning, he laces his fingers with mine and shifts so we're sitting closer together. I could easily lay my head on his shoulder, but I don't let myself. That feels like a step further in our relationship than we're ready for. "Please tell me what you were all enthusiastic about. And stop sitting so weird. My shoulder is right here."

Sighing, I relax against him, both hating and loving how comfortable he is. I could fall asleep if I close my eyes, but there's so much to talk about. "I think we need to set a trap for the saboteurs. Catch them in the act."

"How do we do that?" Jonah suddenly sounds as tired as I feel. Maybe even more so. After the scare at my house last night and our adventures as old people in town today, it has been a long twenty or so hours. "No one has been able to get more than a glimpse of them."

"I think it'll be easier once we know who's behind it all."

Jonah speaks through a yawn. "But we don't know who it is."

"I have my theories," I say through my own yawn. Why are yawns always contagious?

"Which are?"

I close my eyes. "Amateurs."

"That's not a person, June. That's a descriptor."

"Semantics." I adjust my position so I'm more fully pressed against Jonah's side, and he responds by tucking his arm around my back and pulling me in close. A contented sigh escapes me. This is the safest place I've ever been. "Can I stay here forever?" I mumble.

I have no idea if Jonah means it when he sleepily replies, "I would like nothing more."

A girl could get used to waking up in Jonah James's arms. It's not something I *should* get used to, but since I'm already here, I'm going to soak up every minute of this. At some point in the night, we both stretched out along the couch, Jonah behind me with his arms around me in a protective hold. Before we both fell asleep again, he whispered to me in the darkness.

"You are something special, June Harper."

At least I think that's what he said, though I could have been dreaming. I dreamed about Jonah all night, envisioning a life where we grew old together and didn't have wrinkles that fall off because we got them with time, not makeup.

It was one of the best dreams I've ever had and made me realize how much I have come to trust this man. No matter his flaws, he is a good man. Maybe one of the best.

Now, as I lay pressed against his warm chest with my head on his arm, I wonder if I'll ever be content with my fuzzy blankets at home when Jonah makes a much better blanket. He's still sound asleep against my back, his breaths deep and slow, and he smells fresh and clean and manly. I have officially found my new favorite place.

For so long, I've been content—if not happy—on my own, but now I'm questioning if my solitary lifestyle here in Laketown is what I really want. Having a man to support me—physically, emotionally, intellectually—would make so many parts of my life better. And if things between Hank and Bonnie keep escalating the way they have been, I am likely to lose my one and only friend.

Based on some of the pictures I've seen online of their weekend away, they're both pretty smitten with each other; I don't think their relationship is fake anymore. I'm happy for Hank, I really am, but losing him leaves me in a place of uncertainty.

It feels dangerous to want a future with someone like Jonah. Someone whose life is so different from mine, who doesn't have as much stability in his career as he would like. I don't want to live in a place like Los Angeles, but wouldn't he make the city worth at least considering? With his big family, he probably doesn't need a support system the way I'm starting to want one, but what if he did?

What if we could be good for each other?

That's a big question. A *terrifying* question. I've hid behind my fear for years, but I can't do that with Jonah. I either have to let him in or let him go.

Shifting my position so I'm more comfortable, I try not to let my thoughts and questions settle too deeply. I don't need to panic about this. At the store yesterday, he said he wants to see where this goes. He's not asking for forever. Just for *now*.

I can handle now.

Jonah's breathing changes, and he moves behind me, arms loosening around me.

"Good morning," I murmur, feeling awkward now that I'm not the only one aware of our position. I feel like I should say something, but what? "This is nice." *Probably not that.*

He chuckles softly. "For you, maybe. My arm is asleep."

I deflate. "Oh." I'll admit I'm disappointed, but if he doesn't want me here, I can move.

But he laughs again and wraps his arms more securely around me, pulling me in before I can get up. "Ow," he says with a groan.

I wince. "Your head?"

"No, my arm. I told you it was asleep. Now I've got that pins and needles thing happening and would love for you to distract me. I accept kisses or foot massages."

Oh, he's playing a dangerous game here. Face flaming, I do my best to keep my voice steady. "I am not touching your feet."

"Kisses it is, then." With impressive skill, he twists me around so I'm facing him and mere centimeters from his mouth. "May I?"

The raspy question mirrors my own desire, and I lean up to meet him, but the trailer door opens before my lips find his, the open doorway filling the space with blinding sunlight.

Shutting his eyes, Jonah groans and drops his head down to my shoulder. "Richie," he complains. "You have the worst timing."

"Sorry, Jonah. I thought you would be up by now."

Squinting in the brightness, I search the trailer for a clock or my phone but come up empty. "What time is it?"

Richie clears his throat, and he looks unsure how to respond to our current entanglement, his eyes darting everywhere but on us. "Uh, almost ten."

I gasp and sit up. Or, I try to sit up, but Jonah is still holding on to me so I end up tumbling to the floor in a heap, knocking my head when I land.

"Payback for last night," Jonah says with a laugh, but he's already on his feet and taking my hands to help me up. "I don't mean that. I'm sorry. Are you okay?" One hand grazes the now tender spot on my head, while the other presses against my waist.

He's definitely looking at me differently. He still has the same spark of amusement and lightness that he's always had, but there's something warmer in his gaze. Deeper somehow, like before I was only seeing the surface of Jonah James, but at some point he opened a door to his inner workings.

It's too intense to look at for very long, so I nod and excuse myself to the bathroom to give myself a break.

Snatching a tube of toothpaste from the sink, I use my finger to give my teeth a quick scrub and listen to the low rumble of voices on the other side of the door as Jonah and Richie talk. I'm grateful for this moment to myself, though I don't think it will do much to help me work through the serious-type feelings that were creeping up when I woke. The big feelings that are going to change my life one way or another.

I'm not sure I can let myself think about the future right now. I'd rather focus on smaller, more palatable problems. We still have a mystery to solve, and this will be the second day in a row that I haven't opened the store if I don't head back into town and do my actual job. Heh. My job. For the first time since I bought the hardware store, no part of me wants to be behind the counter while the seconds tick by in silent mediocrity, and that's a strange feeling in itself.

Thoughts about my dwindling love for the store feel a bit too connected to my growing interest in Jonah, so I force my focus back to the mystery and what I might have figured out last night.

When I exit the bathroom, Jonah takes his turn, leaving me alone in the trailer with Richie. An awkward silence settles over us as we look at each other. He pats a fist against his thigh, and I look at the foil-covered plates that someone must have brought last night and wonder what's inside, even if it's far too late to eat any of it. We probably missed breakfast here on set, but I bet Jonah could get someone to cook for us. I wonder if Dexter would go get us something if I asked, though I have no idea if he's nearby.

Who am I kidding? Neither Richie nor Dexter is ever far from Jonah. Alone time isn't a real thing for a guy like Jonah, something I need to really consider before I make any plans to leave my life behind for his. If I give this thing between us a shot, that will be my life too.

That's...not something I can think about right now.

Thankfully, Jonah doesn't take long and is back at my side, running a hand through his hair.

"It's the kids," I say right as he opens his mouth to speak.

He frowns. "What about kids?"

"The saboteurs. It's a bunch of teenagers."

Glancing at Richie, Jonah seems to process that for a second before he folds his arms and says, "Explain, please."

"Phil Collins has a teenage nephew. Herman works at the grocery store. Glen has a daughter in high school who sometimes goes on house calls with him. The eggs, the crane, the car, it all makes sense!"

Though he smiles at me, Jonah still looks fully confused. I don't blame him, considering I'm apparently too tired to get my thoughts from my head to my mouth. This would be a lot easier to explain if I had—

"Coffee?" Dexter's voice filters through the open door behind Richie, who steps aside to let Dexter in. Dexter's holding a tray with four cups and has another cup in his hand. "I wasn't sure what you like, June," he says, handing the single cup to Jonah. "So I got a bunch."

"Bless you," I breathe, scanning the labels until I find a mocha. "Jonah, your assistant is absolutely perfect." I could get used to this part of having him around.

As Dexter turns beet red, Jonah drains half his coffee, then says, "I know. He's the best. By the way, Dex, I need you to get me a new phone."

Dexter frowns. "What happened to—oh." He wrinkles his nose as he stares at the shattered phone Jonah holds out to him. "Again?"

Jonah chuckles. "I have a bad habit of putting my foot in the wrong place."

"You're good at that," I say with a grin. It's the same things we said yesterday when we were Martin and Maggie.

"I liked that line better when you called me 'dear,'" Jonah replies, winking at me. Then his eyes slowly make their way down my body, like he's noticing what I'm wearing for the first time. He reaches out and touches the hem of the sweatshirt I put on last night, his smile growing. "It looks good on you." I move to take it off and return it, but he stops me by grabbing my hand. "Keep it."

Heat creeps up my neck. "I can't keep your sweatshirt, Jonah."

"Sure you can." He moves closer, shifting his fingers from the fabric to my waist and leaving the trailer far too warm. "You can have anything you want."

I'm starting to think the only thing I want is him.

Richie clears his throat. "Can we get back to the kids thing?"

Right. Solve the mystery first, flirt with Jonah later.

"I was thinking about all the things that have happened," I say, sipping my coffee with happiness. Dexter made a good choice with this one. "And how there's no pattern to any of it."

"Amateurs," Jonah says, repeating what I told him yesterday.

I nod. "As in people who have no idea what they're doing and don't have a plan. Blowing the yolks out of a bunch of eggs? That's just a weird prank. Stealing random props? Not all that disruptive for a film like this."

"What about what happened to Bonnie?" Jonah asks before draining the rest of his coffee. "That could have been a disaster."

"Same with the tire exploding," Richie throws in.

"Exactly! Those were incredibly dangerous and could have gotten people hurt, and I don't think a rational adult would do something like that if the goal is to get you to leave. Especially when this town needs the money you're bringing in. Everyone is super annoyed by the attention this movie is going to bring to Laketown, but I haven't heard anyone say they actually want the film crew to leave."

Something sparks in Jonah's eyes, and he stands a little taller. "But a kid who hears her electrician dad complaining about the crew might think she's being helpful by taking some of his tools and fraying a couple of wires."

"Yes," I say, pointing at him. "And someone with access to the grocery store's POS system might—"

"Point of sale," Jonah says with a quick glance at Dexter, who looks like he might start giggling. "Not what you're thinking."

Dexter's lips twist up in a grin. "But POS can also mean piece of sh—"

"He could easily put in a fake delivery order," Jonah finishes for me, rolling his eyes. "I think you're on to something, June, but we have no way to prove it. Or to figure out who—ah. Trap." He grins and touches the back of his head. "Now I get it."

"How do you lay a trap for a bunch of teenagers?" Richie asks, folding his arms.

"And why would they go after you the way they did?" Jonah asks me.

"I thought about that a lot last night," I say, relieved that he hasn't called my theory crazy, even if there's a high chance I'm grasping at straws. "And I'm going to guess one of the perpetrators is Scott Packard, the mayor's son. He begged me to hire him at my store a couple of months ago, but it's not like I need the help. He's disliked me ever since, just like Herman, and I know they're friends."

"Herman," Dexter mutters with a snort of laughter. "What a name."

"That's rich coming from a guy named Dexter," Jonah quips back. When he looks at me again, his eyes are bright. "Did you come up with a trap as well?"

This is where things could get fun. "I thought we could play to their advantage."

"How so?"

"You haven't filmed the scene at the school yet, have you?"

Jonah shakes his head. "Not yet."

"But they've been getting one of the classrooms ready," Dexter adds. "To film as soon as Bonnie gets back into town."

That's what I was hoping for, and I start bouncing on my feet despite having no idea if my plan will even work. "Think we could get the crew to pretend they're filming today?"

Humming, Jonah meets Dexter's gaze, and they seem to have a silent conversation before he nods. "Yeah, we probably could. But how will the trap work? The kids would have to know we're doing it, and who's to say they'll even try something?"

I grin wide. "We'll make sure we give them something they can't resist."

CHAPTER SIXTEEN

JUNE

THERE'S A REASON I avoid the diner on Saturdays, and I have to resist the urge to wrinkle my nose when I step through the doors and am bombarded by the noise of what feels like half the town crammed into the small space. I feel dozens of eyes on me—I'm not known for joining town traditions—but I do my best to ignore them as I make my way to the counter to put in an order to go.

Just as I hoped, a large group of teens have gathered in the corner as they often do.

"Fancy seeing you here on a Saturday, June," Peg says by way of greeting. She looks a little overwhelmed by the sheer number of people she and Karina are waiting on, but she smiles at me, which is unexpected. "I heard you were out sick yesterday."

I nod, trying to look tired. Easy enough, considering how much I wish I could go back to Jonah's trailer and spend the day sleeping in his arms. We've only been apart for a couple of hours while we try to get everything ready, but I miss him. A lot. "Yeah, I'm still not feeling great, which is why I'm here to order some soup to bring home."

She looks over the bursting tables and sighs as she picks up a pot of coffee. "Sure thing. Give me a minute?"

I'll give her all the time she needs so my plan can have the best effect. Before I can tell her I'm happy to wait, the bell over the door jingles, and I look over as Dexter comes inside looking like a man with a plan. Ignoring the whispers that start up as people recognize him, he comes over to where I'm standing.

"I need to get a lunch order for my boss ASAP," he tells Peg.

Peg's friendliness vanishes in an instant. "You'll have to wait your turn."

Dexter rolls his eyes and pulls out his phone as Peg heads out to check on her tables and refill coffee mugs.

I chuckle. "Is Jonah James being difficult?"

Feigning surprise, Dexter looks over at me. "Oh, June. Hey. Didn't see you there. Feeling any better? Jonah's been asking about you since you stopped coming around the set, and he was worried when he heard you were sick." For not being an actor, he sounds entirely natural. Maybe some of Jonah's skills have rubbed off on him.

Shrugging, I lean against the counter and turn so I'm facing the group of teens. They're all suddenly very quiet and pretending not to listen, which fuels my conviction that they're behind everything. "I've been better, but I hope I'll be on the mend soon. I've, uh, had some things going on."

"You and Jonah both," Dexter says, his eyes on his phone again. "He's starting to get paranoid about the things happening on set, and it's messing with his head. I don't think he's had a good night's sleep since he got locked in the prop trailer."

I wince. "Yikes. But things always go wrong during filming, right? This is just normal stuff?"

Dexter's lips twitch, and it's a good thing he's not facing the teens because he looks like he might crack. "This is beyond normal," he says darkly. "People are really starting to get freaked out, and the director has been hinting he might move filming back to Hollywood if another thing goes wrong." He looks around and starts tapping his foot impatiently. "Where is that waitress? Jonah needs something to eat before he starts filming at the school in an hour."

I cough to cover a laugh, wishing I could applaud Dexter's delivery. Clear and to the point. I like it. "I'm sure she'll be back in just a minute. I'm in no rush, so you can order ahead of me. Wouldn't want to keep the high and mighty Jonah James waiting."

Peg does indeed return a moment later, and as Dexter places an order for a Caesar salad, the teenagers filter out of the diner one by one.

I'm almost disappointed that every sign is telling me I was right.

"Now that we're here, I'm not so sure this is going to work." I watch the crew put their finishing touches on the set at the high school, though Beckett was only willing to send half the team he would normally use on a scene. Apparently Jonah's persuasive power only went so far to convince the director that my plan would lead to an end of the sabotage. Things are looking a little sparse, and there hasn't been any sign of the kids around the school.

"Everything is going to go great," Jonah says, though he's mostly focused on the phone he borrowed from Richie. When I got to the school after setting the trap at the diner, Jonah said he got a script to look over, and I can't decide if it's a good thing or a bad thing. Jonah's expression is nothing but a mask, though that could be because of Katie styling his hair. We're trying to make this setup look as authentic as possible, though Katie seems to be enjoying herself a little too much while Dexter stands by and offers commentary from a post he just put on Instagram for Jonah.

This is Jonah's life—reading scripts in between takes. Being swarmed by hair and makeup. Getting constant comments from his assistant about messages and social media. It's illuminating to see this side of him, real scene or not, and I try to picture him in this situation all the time when he goes back to California. Jonah likely won't get the chance to give me his full attention very often, and I will have to be okay with that if I decide I want this thing between us to continue after he's gone.

Now that we're almost at the end of all this sabotage nonsense, the future is coming at me faster than I'd like.

Jonah glances up at me and smiles before returning to Richie's phone. It's brief, but it's the kind of smile that warms me inside and out.

I've never been one to need much attention, but I want it. From him. Am I ready to share him with the rest of the world? Do I have a choice? He has implanted himself in my heart, and I'm pretty sure he's there to stay.

"Oh, your publicist wants to video chat in the next day or two," Dexter says while typing on his phone, making Jonah look up again. His eyes jump to me for a second before turning back to Dexter. "And your agent wants that audition sent to her before the end of next week, but I told her—"

"Hold that thought." Jonah gently waves Katie away, pats Dexter on the head, tucks Richie's phone into his pocket, and then he's suddenly right in front of me, wrapping an arm around my waist and pulling me into his chest. "You look worried," he murmurs in my ear. "Why? Your plan will work."

I sigh and melt against him, letting him hold up the weight of my worries. How did he notice that when he barely looked at me? "And if it doesn't work? I think Beckett really will move filming to Los Angeles if things keep happening."

"That's not the end of the world. We've gotten a lot of the exterior shots already, and—"

"And you would be in California."

Jonah has helped me feel confident again. Valuable. *Desired*. He's brought life to my world that I didn't realize was missing until his goodness illuminated the empty corners. And I'm not ready to lose that yet.

His arms pull tighter around me. "Yeah, I would."

Suddenly wanting to change the subject, I slip from Jonah's hold and ask, "How's the script you got? Is it something you're interested in?"

He frowns, though I'm not sure if it's because of my question or because I'm not at his side anymore. "The script is okay. Not my favorite, but..." He shrugs.

"But what?"

"I'll probably take the gig anyway. I generally don't say no to opportunities."

But it kind of sounds like he wants to. "Are you sure?"

"Why would I say no?"

I find myself smiling, suddenly wondering how many of his movies have been projects he disliked. "I mean, I know you want to keep yourself relevant, and I get that, but if you don't like the movie, then don't act in it."

His expression shifts into a mixture of surprise and appreciation, and that is a look I could absolutely get used to. How often does he have someone to talk things through with? Or is he out there making career decisions on his own all the time? It's not that he's not capable, but I know all too well how stressful it can be to make choices without having someone to bounce ideas off of. Before Hank and I became friends, I was on my own when I moved here, and it sucked. My parents, supportive as they are, usually just agreed with anything I said.

I wouldn't be surprised if Jonah's team are the same way.

"It's up to you," I say when he remains silent, "but I think you should do things you want to do."

"I talked to my dad last night." Jonah grabs hold of my hand.

I have no idea how that relates to this conversation, but I am all for hearing more about his family. "Oh?"

He nods and shifts closer, bridging the gap I put between us only moments ago. "He got after me for helping pay for stuff on the farm, and he said some things that…" His eyes jump to the film crew in the room, and something sparks in his eyes. "Come over here."

Tugging me with him, he moves to the back of the classroom, near an open supply closet and far from any of the other people bustling about the room. Once we're alone, he takes hold of my other hand and breathes in deeply, as if to steady himself. "So I talked to my dad," he says again, "and for some reason, something he said has stuck with me all day, and you just reaffirmed what he said, which makes me think it's something I should pay attention to. What if I don't have to cram my year with projects? What if I found a way to give myself some bigger gaps of free time?"

"Alright, people!" Beckett's voice booms through a megaphone, which feels unnecessary given the small space. "*Someone* forgot to bring the props we need for this scene, so let's break for lunch and pick up again in half an hour."

My heart rate kicks up a notch. "Hang on," I whisper, "is the trap being set right now?"

Jonah nods, watching everyone filter out of the room, Beckett included. Richie pauses at the door, his eyes on us, but disappears after a few seconds. We'll need to make ourselves scarce too, but Jonah doesn't seem to be in a hurry. "Security must have noticed someone coming into the school who shouldn't," he mutters. "Looks like the cameras are rolling and ready to go."

"We should go."

"Wait." Jonah's hands tighten around mine. "I might chicken out if I don't get this out now. If I figured out how to take some months off during the year, could I come visit you?"

My breath catches in my throat, and I feel like I just ran an ultramarathon. My heart's pounding so hard that I can hear it in my ears, but I've never been this excited in my life. "Visit?" I breathe.

He leans in until his nose brushes mine. "Date," he amends. "I want to come date you, June. Not just for a couple of weeks. And I know I said I didn't want forever, but I feel like—" He stops, eyes jumping to the ceiling as a scratching sound fills the silent space. "Is that...?"

One of the speckled tiles tilts, slipping from the ceiling, but a hand grasps it and pulls it upward, leaving a gap in the ceiling. A second later, a pair of pristine Nikes appear, followed by two skinny legs that dangle from the hole.

Panicking, I pull Jonah into the closet and grab the door, shutting it as quickly and quietly as I can. "Oh my gosh, are they seriously coming in from the ceiling?" Wishing I had left the door ajar, I press my ear to the door, trying to hear what's happening outside as the lights of the classroom go dark.

"Katie, you go write the message, then watch the door," a young man says, too loudly for someone who's supposed to be sneaking around. I roll my eyes but keep listening. "Herman, you and Nick move all the desks so they're in a circle or something. I'll get the windows."

The sounds of desks and chairs shifting cover up any other conversation that might be happening, but now I know for sure I was right. Katie is Glen's daughter, and I'm pretty sure Nick is Phil's nephew.

Disappointment sinks like a rock in my stomach. I'm glad to get to the end of this, but I wish the kids wouldn't have gotten themselves into trouble like this. I sort of understand their logic—in their eyes, the movie has brought the town nothing but frustration—but there's no way they could have ever gotten the production crew to leave with this half-formed plan of theirs. And what if someone had gotten hurt?

It only takes a few minutes before the room goes silent again, though I still wait a bit in case they come back. When I'm positive the room is empty and the kids have gone, hopefully to be caught by the security guards before they get very far, I grab the door handle.

It doesn't budge.

"Uh oh," I mutter, trying a little harder.

"June," Jonah says. He's been quiet up until now.

"Maybe it's just stuck."

"June, please don't tell me we're locked in here." Jonah's voice sounds almost strangled, and it's only now that I remember he's claustrophobic. "*June.*"

"We might be locked in," I admit, as much as I don't want to.

Jonah groans. Then he swears. "Why do you never charge your phone, Richie?" he growls. "June, do you have—"

"I left my phone out in the classroom."

He swears again, and it sounds like he collides with one of the shelves, though it's too dark to see him. In the next second, he's at my side and banging on the door. "Help!" he shouts, sounding truly terrified.

"Jonah."

"We're stuck! *Help!*"

"Jonah!" Finding his shoulder, I run my hand up until I can press my palm to his cheek. "Jonah, everyone's going to be gone for at least another fifteen minutes."

He groans, pulling away from my touch and disappearing into the darkness. "Fifteen minutes," he says breathlessly. "Do you have any idea how *long* that is?"

"You're okay, Jonah."

He swears again, and then there's a *bang* and it sounds like several books and various objects tumble to the floor. He's going to hurt himself if he's not careful, but I don't know how to help him. Turning back to the door, I feel along the wall to the right of it, hoping to find a light switch. There's nothing, so I try the other side, growing more desperate the longer I hear Jonah struggling to breathe. There *has* to be a light in here, right?

When my search comes up empty, I take a chance and move toward the middle of the tiny space, my hands above my head in the hopes that the school is simply outdated and there's a chain I can pull. My toes collide with something, stopping my forward movement, but I keep waving my hands around until—finally—something cold brushes my fingers. I grasp hold and tug, and a dim orange glow washes over the room.

Jonah is sitting on the floor, elbows on his knees and his arms over his head. Notebooks and binders litter the floor around him, but my focus is on him and the way he seems to be fighting for air. If he panicked after getting stuck in the props trailer, I can only imagine how he's feeling right now with only a few feet of space around him.

"Hey," I say gently, kneeling in front of him.

He doesn't move.

I tuck my hands behind his elbows and pull his arms from his head so I can at least see a part of his face. "Jonah, focus on me, okay? Don't worry about the room. Just look at me."

He peeks up, and though his eyes dart to the door behind me, at least he is in control enough to return his attention to my face. "You make that easy," he mutters, his breathing still erratic. "But I need to get out of here, June."

"I know. And you will." Now that he's looking at me, I grab his ankles next, stretching his long legs out. He barely fits. "But until then, maybe I can distract you." Though he doesn't respond to that, he does seem more focused as he watches me shift forward, putting one leg on either side of his so I can settle myself on his lap.

This isn't how I imagined finally getting a moment alone with Jonah James, but I'll take what I can get.

"You're already doing a great job," he murmurs, moving his hands so one rests on my waist and the other brushes my cheek. His lips twitch up in a smile. "But I could use something a little more...diverting."

Now I'm the one who's nervous. I might have shared a couple of quick kisses with this man, but the way he's looking at me right now is not going to lead to anything quick and simple. Am I ready to fully let go of my fears and open my heart to Jonah? Because if I kiss him—really kiss him—that will open a door I won't be able to close. Reaching up, I brush shaky fingers through his hair. He closes his eyes and shifts his hand from my face to join the other at my back, like he's giving me all the power in this moment. Despite his anxiety, he's still willing to let me go at my own pace.

It's that surrender that gives me the courage to close my eyes and press my lips to his.

Jonah's lips are soft. Warm. And though his hands tighten their grip on me, he does nothing else but meet my tentative kiss with his own. It is gentle and beautiful and not nearly enough. "June," he whispers against my lips.

"What's your real name?" I whisper back.

I feel him smile. "Are you sure you want to know? I told you you'll be disappointed."

"When it comes to you, I don't know if anything can disappoint me."

He kisses me again, then pulls back slightly, his eyes dancing when I look at him. "My name is John."

"John," I repeat, tangling my fingers in his hair again. "That's not all that different from Jonah."

"Maybe not."

"John Martin...what? I'm guessing it's not James."

He shakes his head, his smile growing. "No, it's not. If I tell you my last name, will you let me kiss you properly?"

"That wasn't a proper kiss?" I don't need him to answer that question. Every kiss with Jonah has been amazing, but they have been as tame as kisses can get.

He chuckles. "If that was all I got with you, I would be happy. But no, it wasn't." His hands slide more around me and pull me closer. "I am so ready to really kiss you, June Harper."

I bite my lip. "First tell me your full name."

"John." He brushes a kiss against the corner of my mouth. "Martin." Kisses the other corner. "*Smith.*"

My gasp is swallowed up as he captures my mouth with his, not with a sweet, simple kiss but with the kind of kiss that leaves me breathless. His hands jump to my head, pulling me in as his mouth moves against mine, over and over again in the most delicious way. But I can tell he's holding back, and I am not going to walk out of this closet regretting what could be my best chance to fully kiss Jonah James. *John.*

"Mr. Smith," I say with a little laugh, then claim his mouth for my own, tucking my arms around his neck and taking command. Jonah responds eagerly, matching everything I do with leashed enthusiasm, letting me decide each step in a way no one has ever done before. The level of respect and adoration is enough to completely silence my thoughts and worries.

But I'm ready to set him free.

"Kiss me," I whisper.

With a breathless laugh, Jonah does as I ask, tugging me closer and kissing me deeper until I *really* can't think straight. His hands are on my waist, in my hair, running down my back, while I explore his chest, his shoulders, anywhere I can touch. He kisses as confidently as he does everything else, and I will never get enough.

"Jonah?"

I gasp and break away from Jonah at the sound of Richie's voice, though I'm surprised I heard it. The closet door is still closed, but light spills from underneath.

"Jonah!" Richie calls again, sounding frantic now.

I move to get up, but Jonah's arms tighten around me, and he gives me a warning look. "What happened to wanting to get out of here?" I ask with a chuckle.

He shakes his head, a flash of fear warring with the desire in his eyes. "Not yet."

I think he knows as well as I do that as soon as we get rescued, it could be a long time before we're ever alone again. Surely this can't be the only chance we get, can it? A lifetime of always having Richie or Dexter or a stranger right there to keep us apart? It would be hard enough for *me* to be in the tabloids like Hank, but can Jonah really live in the spotlight for the rest of his life? I don't think he minds that part, and it comes with his job, so... Reality is never going to change, even if he does cut back on projects. Choosing to be with him means choosing to sacrifice the quiet life I've built for myself.

Jonah buries his hand in my hair, pulling my head down until my forehead rests against his. "We can figure this out," he says, as if he read all my worries on my face. "It might not be easy, but we can make it work."

"How?" I whisper, curling myself up against him and burying my face in his neck. "Jonah—John—what do I even call you now?"

Though a commotion starts up outside, probably the production team realizing no one can find Jonah, Jonah tucks his arms around me in the most protective hold I've ever felt. "Honestly, I prefer Jonah. It's been my name almost as long as John was. And it's the name that brought me to you."

Okay, I love that. But I still need to know how we're going to go forward. "Jonah. As much as I want to say I'd be fine, I don't think I can live in Los Angeles."

"I know."

"And you can't live in Laketown."

He hums and runs his hand up and down my back in a soothing motion. "Not all the time," he agrees. "And I would hate it every time I had to leave. But I would keep coming back, June."

"That's crazy. You can't spend your life in two different places, always on the move."

For some reason, that makes him laugh, and he presses a kiss to my forehead. The sounds in the classroom have grown quiet, and I'm going to guess everyone is out looking for us now. "That's already how I live my life, June. And for you, I would do whatever it takes to make it work. You have grounded me in a way nothing ever has, and suddenly I don't feel like I'm drifting aimlessly and reaching for something I can't even see. I feel like I have a...a *reason*, you know? You have no idea how important that makes you."

Goodness, this man knows his way around words. Sniffling, I press a hand to his chest, feeling the way his heart beats so steadily when mine feels erratic and uncertain. Jonah has always been a confident man, but I can't fathom how he's so confident about us.

"Look," Jonah says, his hand at my back growing still. "It won't be easy. For either of us. You've had it rough, and I'm nowhere near perfect. I will never do what your ex did to you, but I'm bound to be an idiot now and then."

I let out a little laugh. "That I believe."

"But I'm not looking for something temporary."

My breath hitches.

"And I'm not afraid of hard work."

I lift my head to look him in the eyes.

His expression is full of determination. "June, we'll take this thing one day at a time, but I'm in this for the long haul. As long as you'll have me."

There's so much I don't know how to navigate—the distance, his fame, my realization that I'm not as tied to Laketown as I thought—but right now, I want to follow Jonah's lead and take things one step at a time.

"Okay," I whisper, brushing my fingers through his hair. "Let's see where this goes."

Jonah's face lights up in the most beautiful way, so much brighter than the pitiful bulb above us. He's always been a happy guy, but this is next level. "June Harper," he says before pressing his lips to mine.

Who needs to get out of this closet? Not me.

The strangest sound pulls us apart again, and while Jonah groans in frustration, I turn to look at the door, as if I might be able to see what in the world made that noise on the other side.

"There it is again," I whisper as a *yowl* comes through the door. A second later, a fuzzy orange paw pokes through the crack at the bottom, and my jaw drops. "No way."

"Is that Samson?" Jonah asks, peering around my shoulder. "In the *high school*?"

Samson yowls again, his paw wiggling around like he's trying to figure out how to get the door open.

"How?" I ask and climb off of Jonah's lap so I can inch closer to the door. "Hey, kitty kitty. What are you doing here?" His yowling changes to the softest, sweetest, meow I've ever heard, like he's suddenly a different cat. Though I'm likely to get stabbed by his massive claws, I reach out and touch a finger to the pink pad on his foot.

His claws retreat at the same time his toes curl around my finger.

I gasp at the feel of his fur, so much softer than I would have expected from a stray cat. This is the first time he's ever let me touch him, and while it's likely because he doesn't realize it's me, I still feel like the universe has made a shift in my favor.

I only get to hold his paw for a few seconds before his arm disappears, but then the handle to the closet jiggles. My eyebrows shoot high as I stand. "Is that the cat trying to open—"

"Hey!" Jonah says, scrambling forward until he's at my side. "We're trapped in here!"

"Jonah?" Richie's voice is filled with relief. Right. Of course it wasn't Samson trying to open the door. "The door is locked."

"The key might be in the teacher's desk," I say, hoping I'm not giving Jonah false hope by saying something that isn't true.

Except, now that he's next to me, Jonah doesn't seem all that concerned about getting the door open. His eyes are fixed on me, dark and burning, and he snakes his arm around my waist to pull me flush against his body.

"This could be your last chance to kiss me without an audience for a while," I murmur, gripping his strong biceps.

"Not if I have anything to say about it." He twists us around so I'm pressed against the door, and then he kisses me with renewed vigor, his exploration thorough and filled with heat.

The door opens behind me. I stumble and fall, Jonah coming with me, and land on my back with an *oof* as his weight settles over me.

"Jonah?"

Jonah lifts his head and playfully scowls at his bodyguard. "Richie, we seriously need to work on your timing. You couldn't have waited thirty more seconds?"

"Five more minutes?" I breathlessly counter.

Laughing, Jonah gets to his feet and helps me up. As soon as I'm on my feet, he pulls me into his arms and holds on tight. "I promise," he whispers into my ear. "We'll get time."

Time together, time alone, time in the future. I want it all.

Something brushes against my leg, and I look down in surprise. Sure enough, Samson is rubbing himself against me like it's the most normal thing in the world.

"Looks like someone finally came to his senses," Jonah murmurs.

"Is the cat part of the prank?" Beckett asks.

That's when I realize just how many people are in the room, though I'm guessing there are still a few out looking for us in the school. Most of the crew looks unsure about what they should be doing, which means they're all just staring at Jonah and me.

"What in the world?" Jonah says, his eyes flitting about the room.

As I look around, I fully understand his confusion. The kids' idea of a high school haunting was arranging the desks so they all face the camera at the back of the room. Someone wrote "LEAVE" in capital letters on the chalkboard, the lines harsh and messy, and the windows are all open to let in a breeze. And one of the overhead lights is flickering more than before, but not in a creepy way. Just an annoying little blip every couple of seconds.

That last bit probably isn't part of the prank at all.

"Did we catch them?" Jonah asks, mainly to Beckett.

The director sighs and folds his arms. "Got them on their way out a back door, and we're sending the footage to the mayor as proof. All four of the kids had clear shots of their faces within the first thirty seconds. I thought this whole idea was stupid, but apparently the kids were stupider."

"I think in this case they were desperate," I say and turn to Jonah. "Hopefully this means the rest of the movie will go without a hitch."

"There's no such thing," he replies, kissing my cheek. "But I think things will be smoother."

"Let's get this set fixed now that our leading man is no longer missing," Beckett says, waving to the crew. As they start rearranging the desks again, he shifts closer to us and drops his voice as he speaks to Jonah. "Then everyone's getting a few days off. Bonnie won't be back until Tuesday anyway, and I need to spend some time in civilization. I'm going to turn off my phone, drive to Sun City, find a real restaurant, and then take the world's longest nap."

"That sounds like a great idea," Jonah says. "You could use a break after all this." But then his eyes shift to me, his expression turning heated. "I think we could all use a few days of alone time."

Yes please. I slip my hand into his and take a deep breath, letting the last of my worries melt away as I exhale. I don't know what my life is going to look like after the next few days, but I don't really care. Right now, all I care about is enjoying my time with Jonah James while I've got it.

EPILOGUE

JONAH

Three months later

"Could you go any faster?" I bounce my leg, doing my very best not to reach over and push the gas pedal myself. I usually don't mind how intently Richie adheres to speed limits, but today is not the day for meandering. "Seriously, how slow are you going?" I lean over to see the speedometer, but Richie pushes me away.

"Stop distracting the driver," he grumbles.

"Stop driving like a ninety-year-old woman," I grumble back.

Glancing at me out of the corner of his eye, he eases off the gas enough for me to notice us slowing down.

I point a finger at him. "So help me, Richard Prince, if you don't get me to Laketown in the next five minutes, I'm going to fire you and hire a Formula 1 driver to replace you."

"No, you won't."

He's right. Richie was one of the best things to ever happen to me, and I would be lost without his friendship. Especially lately. Over the last two and a half months, he has been the only thing keeping me sane while I've been filming in Los Angeles.

But I have my first free weekend in weeks, and I don't want to waste a minute of it.

When Laketown comes into view seven minutes later, I'm a giant ball of nerves. June doesn't know I caught an earlier flight, so she won't be expecting me for another three hours. Video chats and phone calls have been great, but I'm still worried she won't react to my surprise appearance the way I want her to. What if she has just been humoring me? No matter how many times she says she misses me, she seems pretty content most days. Business has picked up at her store since the day a tabloid story went out after someone figured out June and I are dating. She's been spending a lot of time with Hank and helping him get ready to move to Los Angeles to be with Bonnie. And now that Samson has decided he likes June, she has a cuddle buddy most nights, so she doesn't even need me.

Richie parks in one of the few open spots on Main Street, just down the street from June's store. I don't move an inch, and that seems to be the straw that breaks the camel's back and forces him to the end of his patience with me. "Don't you dare," he growls, reaching over and unlatching my seatbelt. "I did not spend the last two months listening to you moan and mope just to have you sit here and pretend you're not dying to see June." He grumbles something about how much complaining I've done in the last two hours alone during the drive from the airport in Sun City. "And now you're just going to sit here?"

I grimace. "Of course I want to see June. But what if she doesn't want to see me?"

Richie undoes his own seatbelt and climbs out of the car, stalking around to my door and wrenching it open. "*Go,*" he snaps. "I'll be waiting outside."

"You're being irrational," I mutter to myself as I slip from the car and straighten my t-shirt. I'm already sweaty, as much from nerves as from the summer heat, and the longer I take to find the courage to go inside the hardware store, the worse it will be. I'm more nervous now than I was for our first date; there's so much more at stake now.

When I met June, I was fueled by curiosity. Now I'm fueled by a bone-deep need to be in her life.

By the time I finally step through the door of June's store, knocking the bell overhead and making it jingle, I feel like I should take a quick detour to the bed and breakfast and shower before making this reunion happen. June would never know I got here early, and maybe I wouldn't be so...

All of my anxiety melts away the moment I see June talking to her teenage employee, Scott—the mayor's son. He started working for her as part of his community service hours while the other kids helped on set, but when things picked up after the tabloid article, she decided to hire him. Not only does it mean she has help during the busy weekends, but she's also been able to take more afternoons off, using the time to chat with me or update parts of her house she's been wanting to remodel since she bought the place.

She's more beautiful than she ever has been, and I can't seem to move from my spot in the doorway.

When the door closes behind me, ringing the bell again, June looks over. Goes still. Her expression is blank, leaving me to wonder if coming here at all was a good idea.

I swallow the lump in my throat. "Hey."

Dropping the box of nails she was holding, June rushes forward and throws her arms around my shoulders. I wrap her up, relishing the feel of her in my arms. I feel like I've had a hole in my chest since the day I had to head back to California, and she is the only thing that can fill it.

"You're really here," she breathes, burying her face in my neck.

"I'm here," I reply. And I don't know how I'm going to convince myself to leave again now that I am. I tighten my hold as tears well up in my eyes. "You have no idea how much I've missed you, June Harper."

"Not more than I've missed you."

I reluctantly loosen my grip as she pulls away, and I take her in. She's wearing the same apron she wore on the day I met her, and in the strangest way it almost makes it feel like it hasn't been months since I last held her in my arms. Since I last kissed her.

She must have been reading my thoughts because she leans up on her toes and presses her lips to mine. The kiss is simple and sweet, but I can feel the promise of more. "Let me just make sure Scott is good to close up, okay?"

I agree to let her leave my arms only because it means she and I can go somewhere more private.

Two months and eighteen days is too long to go without time alone with June Harper.

June

Two months later

"I feel underdressed." I brush a hand over my ruffled tank top, wishing I had chosen to wear a skirt or something instead of distressed jean shorts. When Jonah picked me up from the Boise airport this morning, I thought we would stop at the hotel instead of driving directly to his parents' farm. But now we're standing outside the cutest farmhouse I've ever seen, complete with a wraparound porch, painted yellow shutters, and flower boxes teeming with multi-hued blooms. Richie already went inside, so we won't be able to make an escape and pretend we couldn't make it. "Jonah, I can't show up to your dad's seventy-fifth birthday party looking like this! What will your mother think?"

Slipping his hand into mine, he leans down and kisses my temple. "She'll wonder how I managed to snag someone so entirely out of my league. We can sneak upstairs so you can change if you want, but I guarantee at least three people will see you as you are. Besides, you look amazing." He kisses me again, lingering this time. "Mm. How do you always smell this good?"

If anyone smells good, it's him. It's been long enough since he was last in Laketown that I almost forgot how much I love burrowing into his chest and breathing him in. Whatever cologne he uses, it mixes with his natural scent and leaves him mouthwatering.

Leaning into him, I rise on my toes and tease a kiss against his lips. "I like the sound of sneaking upstairs."

He groans and captures my mouth with a kiss almost as good as the one he gave me when we first found each other at the airport. "You're going to get me in trouble," he murmurs against my mouth as his thumb brushes a spot of bare skin at my waist, leaving a trail of heat in its wake.

"Good," I say and tug him back into the kiss.

A throat clearing pulls us apart.

Two men stand on the porch with matching smirks, their arms folded and mischief in their eyes. Though I've seen pictures, I can't tell which brother is which because the whole family looks so alike. "Hey, Hollywood," the one on the right says. "Are you going to come inside, or is making out on the front lawn your only goal for this weekend?"

"This is why I don't let my kids watch your movies," the other one says, shaking his head.

Jonah snorts and gives me a questioning look that is easy to read. When I nod, he claims my mouth again, leaning so deep into the kiss that I get weak in the knees. It's not that I *want* to be kissing like this in front of his family, but he is giving me an extremely convincing argument for not caring at all what they witness.

"Okay, Casanova," one of the brothers says, louder than before. "Mom is dying to meet your lady friend."

"I'm your lady friend?" I ask with a breathless laugh.

Jonah chuckles. "You are so much more than that," he murmurs with another kiss, then turns to his brothers. "And would you lay off, Steve? I haven't seen her in months."

"Sounds like a personal problem."

It *is* a personal problem. It was hard enough when Jonah left Laketown the first time, but watching him drive away after he spent a weekend with me earlier this summer was so much harder than I thought it would be. Every video call since then has only somewhat lessened the loneliness I've been feeling lately. Samson is great company now that he has decided to be an indoor cat, but his cuddling doesn't come close to being in Jonah's arms.

Long distance is better than nothing, but there has to be a better way to do this. Jonah has been scaling back his availability, much to the dismay of his agent, but from what I can tell, he's becoming more of a hot commodity now that he isn't agreeing to every job he can. Studios are willing to pay more for him, and once *Frosted Peaks* comes out in a few months and everyone sees just how good of an actor he is when he gets the right chance, his value will only go up.

I'm hoping that means he'll be able to take even more time off.

Jonah's brothers head inside, leaving the door wide open, and I take the hint. "I guess I'm not going to change," I say as my nerves start building again. "You promise I'm not dressed too casually?"

Taking my hand once more, Jonah leads me up the stairs to follow his brothers inside. "It's August in Idaho. I guarantee you are more dressed up than half the family, and no one will be paying attention to your clothes in the first place. They're all going to be wondering how I got so lucky."

He's not the lucky one. I am. And as the Smiths welcome me in with open arms, his mom even tearing up as she gives me a hug, I get my first real taste of a close-knit family. I love my parents, and they have always been on my side. But when it's always been just the three of us, I've been missing a true community.

Jonah's family makes me feel like I'm one of them instantly, and I am going to hold on to this for as long as I possibly can.

Three months later

"Jonah! Over here!"

"Can we get a smile?"

"Jonah!"

"Jonah, who's your date tonight?"

The cameras keep flashing, and I'm pretty sure I'm going to be blind before the night is over. This isn't even the actual premiere for *Frosted Peaks*—I chickened out and skipped that one a few nights ago—but tonight's watch party event is still way bigger than anything I've ever attended.

"You're doing great," Jonah says through a broad smile. "We're almost done."

Easy for him to say. He's been through this dozens of times and has the personality of a golden retriever, so everyone is always excited to see him. These movie premieres and watch parties are actually fun for him.

But me? I'm blind, in a dress, and desperate to hear him answer the question we're hearing most often tonight: "Who is that next to you?"

With this being my first official public outing with the charming Jonah James, I really want to know what he'll say. Now that I've decided to make an appearance, our relationship isn't tabloid gossip anymore. It'll be a lot harder to hide after tonight.

We finally move on from the photographers, Jonah tugging me along with his hand laced with mine, and pause in front of a gorgeous woman standing in front of a video camera with a microphone. Jonah warned me we would have to stop and talk to at least some of the reporters here tonight, but he promised he would pick the nice ones. This one looks kind enough, though they're all a little terrifying.

"Jonah James!" the reporter says, her smile bright and genuine. Her eyes jump to me for half a second, but she keeps her focus on Jonah, for which I'm grateful. I'm happy to be a background fixture as I try to figure out how anyone can smile for this long without their lips falling off. "Are you riding high on the success of *Frosted Peaks*? It was a record-breaking opening weekend."

I can practically feel Jonah's excitement through our connected hands.

"I am blown away by the reception so far," he says, speaking loudly to be heard over the shouts from the paparazzi behind us. They're going nuts over something. Probably Bonnie and Hank, who arrived soon after we did. "This whole project was a labor of love, and I could not be more grateful that everything has turned out better than I could have hoped." He squeezes my hand, the gesture speaking volumes.

I love seeing him in his element. I love more the way he hasn't abandoned me or forgotten me even once, no matter how many people are vying for his attention.

"Your character is only in the first book," the reporter says. "What are the chances we might see more of Logan Banks in the movies?"

Jonah chuckles, shaking his head. "There's no way we would stray from the genius of Henry McAllister's writing, no matter how much I would love to work on the series more. Think anyone would notice if I auditioned for Hudson Bluth in the next movie?"

The reporter laughs, and then her attention finally turns to me. "June," she says, because of course she knows my name, "I have to ask. What's it like dating someone who is quickly becoming one of the best actors in Hollywood?"

Jonah ran through some of the questions I might get asked tonight, and I'm so glad this was on his list because I have a ready answer prepared. "I wouldn't know," I say, leaning into the microphone. "For me, Jonah is just a regular guy, and I sometimes forget he's famous because when we're together, he's the same cheesy dork he was when I met him."

"June is the best thing to ever happen to me," Jonah says and kisses my temple. "She keeps me grounded, and I can't imagine life without her anymore."

"Good answer," I murmur, beaming up at him.

The interviews continue as we make our way down the red carpet, all of them much like the first, until the last one, when the reporter asks Jonah if they'll be seeing more of me now that our relationship is out in the public.

"Our relationship is and always will be private," Jonah says without hesitation, and my heart melts. "I'll love those days when June is willing to join me here in Hollywood, but I'll always love more when it's just the two of us together. She's my home, and that's not something I'm willing to share."

Dang. I'm left just as speechless as the guy with the microphone, and I'm pretty sure I'm about to start crying because that was the most perfect response I've ever heard.

"I have to like him, don't I?" a soft voice says behind me, and I turn to find Hank, who must have gone ahead of Bonnie because she's deep in conversation with a reporter and Derek Riley of all people. That explains the paparazzi chaos, if Derek is here. "Jonah James is a good guy, isn't he?"

I tuck an arm around Hank as we both watch Jonah continue to discuss the movie. It sounds like he's shut down any more talk about our relationship, and I've never liked Jonah more. "He's kind of the best," I say with a lovesick sigh.

Hank chuckles and returns my side hug. "I'll admit I was pleasantly surprised by his performance in the end."

I smirk. "You loved him. Admit it."

"He wasn't as good as Bonnie."

"You are way too biased to make that claim, McAllister. Of course you think your wife was a better actor than my..."

Hank raises an eyebrow. "Than your what?"

I look at Jonah again, who seems to feel my gaze because he turns right then and sends me a smile that warms me from my head to my toes. I don't know what kind of label to put on him, but I don't care. He's mine, and that's all that matters.

"Why did we get ourselves mixed up in this madness?" I ask instead of answering the question. "We gave up our quiet lives for what?"

Hank laughs and reaches out his hand as Bonnie approaches, her smile wide. "For love," he says simply and follows his wife down the red carpet.

"For love," I repeat, feeling my own grin stretch as Jonah looks back at me again.

Definitely for love.

Jonah

Three months later

This might be the first year I don't care about not being nominated for any Oscars. Most years, I sit on my couch in sweats and eat an entire pizza in misery, wondering if I'll ever be the one making faces at the camera as I wait to see if I'll be the next one standing on the stage, holding a golden statue.

This year, I'm cuddled up with June on her couch, Samson asleep on my legs and Hank's latest book open on June's Kindle between us. Richie is out on a date, of all things, which makes everything about tonight feel so different from my usual day-to-day. So normal.

I wish we were doing something else, though. Because filming for my last project ended early, I've been in Laketown for two weeks already, but I never feel like I get enough time with June. I try not to waste what time we do get. Not that reading is a waste of time, but I prefer other activities. Still, June was excited to read the final version of the book, and I'm man enough to admit I'm almost as interested as she is. My character may have only been in the first book, but I'm dying to know how the series is going to end.

"Oh my gosh," June says in a low voice, probably so she doesn't wake the cat. "How are you this slow of a reader?"

I dig my fingers into her side, teasing a giggle out of her before I tap the Kindle to turn the page. "Maybe I'm just trying to draw out the suspense."

"The whole point of suspense is the pacing, but if you're going to read at a snail's pace, then I'm going to pull it up on my phone and read it by myself."

"But then you'll spoil the ending for me!" I complain.

I'm not really complaining. June could tell me flat out how the book ends, and I would still love her more than anything.

"Tell you what," I say, shifting in my seat so I can pull her closer and get in a better position. Samson opens his ugly yellow eyes to glare at me, but he's quick to fall back asleep on my legs. "You read at the pace you want, and if I miss things, you'll just have to fill me in."

She tilts her head up and kisses my jaw. "You would hate that."

"I couldn't possibly hate anything that you do."

"You hate when I don't answer your texts within thirty seconds," she argues.

"Well yeah, because sometimes I only have a couple of minutes in between takes, and I don't want to miss any chance to talk to you." Seeing her name on my phone will never get old, though. The only thing better than getting a text or a phone call is a moment like this, when I can be at her side and breathe in her beauty and goodness and sweet scent that will always be my favorite smell.

It's going to take a couple of years to get to a point where I can spend the majority of my time away from Los Angeles, but I'm feeling more optimistic than I ever have. No matter how chaotic and stressful it's been, the last year of shifting my priorities has given me hope for the kind of future I really want.

Picking up the Kindle, June sets it on the cushion next to her and sits up so she can look at me. "I don't like missing chances either," she says, brushing her hand through my hair. "Which is why I've been thinking about something for a while that I want to run by you. Your mom loves the idea, and I'm hoping you do too."

Interesting. I am nosy enough when it comes to June that I've made sure I'm the first person she tells things to, and while I love that she trusts my mom, I don't know how I feel about not being the first in the know with whatever this is. "Tell me," I say, lifting her fingers to my lips.

June's face turns a light shade of pink, which only intrigues me more. "Okay, so you know that house on the end of your parents' lane?"

I sit up so fast that I get a leg full of claws when Samson startles and leaps from my lap. "Are you about to say what I think you're about to say?" Because I've been eyeing that house ever since it went on the market, but I've been too much of a chicken to mention it to June.

She grins and presses her palm to my cheek. "Sometimes it's creepy how quickly you pick up on things, Jonah James."

"But what about your store? This house?" I'm jumping to conclusions, but I can't help myself. I've been spending half my free time here in Laketown and the other half in Idaho, but every time I'm there I want to be here, and every time I'm here a part of me wants to be with my family. Mom's doing better, but everyone always looks so much older whenever I get the chance to visit.

I feel like I'm missing so much.

Her smile growing, June runs her thumb over my lips. "I've already sold the store, and this house is ready to go on the market as soon as I know if you want me to—"

"You want to move to Idaho? What about work? What about your parents?" I can barely bring myself to breathe.

"My dad is retiring next year, and they're talking about downsizing. Maybe even looking at places in Idaho. And I've been applying for some paralegal jobs."

My thoughts are working too fast for me to keep up. She already sold her store? Is applying for jobs? That means she isn't just thinking about moving closer to my family. She's doing it. "Are you serious about this?" I whisper, gripping her hand tightly. "June, if you moved to Idaho, I wouldn't have to..." Heck, I might never go back to California. Who needs a career, anyway?

There's a light in her eyes now, and she runs her thumb along my lips once more before leaning in and kissing me softly. "Jonah, you've sacrificed sleep and money to jump back and forth between everything, and I love you for that. It's my turn to make a sacrifice, though being close to your family isn't a sacrifice. I love your family almost as much as I love you."

I pull her in for another kiss, losing myself in the taste of her as my heart seems to grow until it's too big for my chest. "I don't deserve you," I whisper against her mouth. "But there is no world in which I will stop you from making this decision if that's what you want. Having you and our families all in the same place..." I didn't know a feeling this big could exist, and I almost don't know what to do with it. "June Harper, you are an exquisite human being."

She kisses me in a way that feels like she's telling me something. If that something means she's willing to stick around for good, it might be time to finish the conversation I started with her mom a few weeks ago and figure out what kind of ring June would like best.

I am so ready to turn one day at a time into the rest of forever.

The End

Be sure to check out Hank and Bonnie's story in *Lovestruck*.

ALSO BY Dana LeCheminant

Starstruck Love Stories

Moonstruck

Lovestruck

Thunderstruck

Dumbstruck

Awestruck

Wonderstruck

Love in Sun City

Kiss Me if You Can

She Likes It, Hey Micah

The Chad Next Door

Crossing the Brooklyn Briggs

Houston, We Have a Problem

Standalone Romances
For Butter or For Worse

The Wonder Boys
Love on Camera
Love in Writing
Love on Display
Love in Disguise

Simple Love Stories (Sweet Love Stories)
Simplicity
Growing Young
Bittersweet Brews
In Front of Me
As Long as You Love Me
Dear Dalia
Let Go

Terms of Inheritance (Sweet Romance)
Forever You and Me
Holding On to Everything
A World without You
Love, Strictly Speaking

Historical Romances
The Thief and the Noble
A Twist of Christmas (part of The Holly and the Ivy anthology)
What Dreams May Come
This above All
Never Doubt I Love

ABOUT THE AUTHOR

Dana LeCheminant has been telling stories since she was old enough to know what stories were. After spending most of her childhood reading everything she could get her hands on, she eventually realized she could write her own books too, and since then she always has plots brewing and characters clamoring to be next to have their stories told. A lover of all things outdoors, she finds inspiration while hiking the remote Utah backcountry and cruising down rivers. Until her endless imagination runs dry, she will always have another story to tell.

Dana loves connecting with her readers! You can find her on social media (**@authordanalecheminant**) and on her website, **lecheminan tbooks.com**.

www.ingramcontent.com/pod-product-compliance
Lightning Source LLC
Chambersburg PA
CBHW060316310726
48976CB00007B/2350